D0035490

"I have no intention of marrying you!"

Instead of answering her protest by telling her why he'd told this latest lie, Severo denied it.

"I may have stretched the truth here and there," he told her coolly, "but I certainly wasn't lying when I said I would be marrying Regina Barrington on the twenty-fourth of this month."

Reggie was shaken rigid, for there was a conviction about him that said he meant every word.

"But...but I never said I'd marry you!" she denied.

Severo flattened her composure before it could get a firm hold. "A girl calling herself Regina Barrington did."

"You mean Bella agreed to marry you?" she gasped, her disbelief clearly evident.

"It would appear that your sister misled you in more than one detail...."

JESSICA STEELE
is also the author of these
Harlequin Romances

Many of these titles are available at your local bookseller.

For a free catalogue listing all available Harlequin Romances
and Harlequin Presents, send your name and address to:

HARLEQUIN READER SERVICE,
1440 South Priest Drive, Tempe, AZ 85281
Canadian address: Stratford, Ontario N5A 6W2

Innocent Abroad

by

JESSICA STEELE

Harlequin Books

TORONTO • LONDON • LOS ANGELES • AMSTERDAM
SYDNEY • HAMBURG • PARIS • STOCKHOLM • ATHENS • TOKYO

Original hardcover edition published in 1981
by Mills & Boon Limited

ISBN 0-373-02446-0

Harlequin edition published December 1981

Copyright © 1981 by Jessica Steele.
Philippine copyright 1981. Australian copyright 1981.

All rights reserved. Except for use in any review, the reproduction or utilization
of this work in whole or in part in any form by any electronic, mechanical or
other means, now known or hereafter invented, including xerography,
photocopying and recording, or in any information storage or retrieval system,
is forbidden without the permission of the publisher, Harlequin Enterprises
Limited, 225 Duncan Mill Road, Don Mills, Ontario, Canada M3B 3K9. All the
characters in this book have no existence outside the imagination of the
author and have no relation whatsoever to anyone bearing the same name
or names. They are not even distantly inspired by any individual known
or unknown to the author, and all the incidents are pure invention.

The Harlequin trademark, consisting of the words HARLEQUIN ROMANCE
and the portrayal of a Harlequin, is registered in the United States Patent
Office and in the Canada Trade Marks Office.

Printed in U.S.A.

CHAPTER ONE

TIGHTLY controlled, Reggie Barrington let herself into the flat she shared with her sister. She closed the door behind her; then, the world shut out, her face crumpled, a deep shuddering breath, and she burst into tears.

The evening she had been so keyed up about, had looked forward to with growing excitement since Clive's telephone call that morning, had not turned out at all as she had anticipated.

They had been dating each other for two months and though she never saw him on Mondays, since yesterday had been such a wonderful day, a day when they had confessed their love for each other, a day that had a dreamlike quality about it, she hadn't been too surprised that he should ring her at the office this morning.

Clive worked on the technical side of an electronics company, and her heart had sunk when after the joy of hearing his eager, 'Do you still feel the same way about me?' her own voice taking on a softness as she'd replied, 'Yes,' he had gone on to tell her he had bad news. His firm had pulled off a terrific deal in the States for some equipment, but one of the technicians who had gone with the team ready to have the equipment working by the new year had fallen ill, and Clive was flying out tomorrow as a replacement. He would be away a whole month, returning on the first of January.

'But you'll be away for Christmas!' The protest had left her feeling that in big business small things like a man wanting to spend the festive season with his loved ones didn't seem to matter. 'You'll miss Bella's wedding!'

'I know, darling.' Clive had sounded pulled two ways, and she had felt pangs of guilt that she was being unreasonable, especially when he added, 'But it will give my career a terrific boost.'

And then he had said something that had sent her disappointment flying, had set her heart thumping so she could hardly answer.

'I know we don't usually see each other on Mondays—but could we make an exception tonight?' She would have been agreeable for no other reason than that if she wasn't going to see him for another month then she just had to see him that night, but when he'd said, 'There's something I want to ask you. Something I want you to think seriously about while I'm away,' she had just known he was going to ask her to marry him.

She had wanted to say straight away that she didn't have to think about it for a month, for a day or even a minute. She could give him his answer now. Of course she would marry him.

It was her old-fashioned upbringing that had held her back from rushing into impulsive speech. Had Gran been alive she would have said, 'Wait till you're asked, girl.'

A loud sob echoing round the tiny flat intruded on her grief, bringing her back to the present, making her aware by the inanimate objects around her that life went on. The hands on the clock on top of the small bookcase were telling her it had gone midnight and that any minute now Bella would be home.

Hastily Reggie dabbed at her eyes and blew her nose. She didn't want Bella to know she had been crying. Not that she would be able to keep from her that she was upset. They had always been close, had drawn closer together when their parents had died and they had gone to live with their grandparents. They confided everything to each other—but oh, how she wished now she had kept back the certainty that was in her that Clive was going to ask her to marry him.

Bella had been busy dressing to go out with James Usher, the man she was to marry on Boxing Day, but she had paused in her preparations on seeing her sister donning her very best dress.

'Hello—what's this?' she had queried, bubbling over with her own happiness after what could only be called a fraught on-off courtship, James' possessiveness being the cause of many an argument when at variance with the streak of independence both girls shared.

'Oh, Bella!' Reggie hadn't been able to hold back, having previously explained that she was seeing Clive tonight because tomorrow he would be going away for a whole month. 'I think Clive is going to propose tonight!'

Bella's shriek of pleasure had only added to her excitement, and now, Reggie thought, going to the minute bathroom to sluice her face, she would have to tell Bella that marriage wasn't what Clive had proposed at all.

She was in bed when she heard Bella's key in the door. She had left the light on knowing she would be eager to know everything. She was. Reggie sat up, her hands clenched as her beautiful blonde sister burst into the room, rendering a loud version of the Wedding March.

Her singing broke off abruptly, one look at Reggie's face speaking volumes. 'Oh, love,' she cried, hurrying over to sit on her bed, 'what happened?'

'Bella! Oh, Bella!' Tears spurted from Reggie's eyes again. 'H-he's—Clive's already—married!'

Bella was so sweet to her after that Reggie was sure no one had a better sister. She insisted on making her a warm drink, then bit by tiny bit got everything out of her. And some twenty minutes later, with a hard look in her eyes that would have boded no good at all for Clive Walker had he been anywhere near, she neatly summed up everything Reggie had told her.

'So this something special he had to ask you was not to marry him, but to go and live with him.'

'He wants to marry me,' Reggie whispered, having heard one or two short sharp things Bella had to say on the subject of the man she had given her heart to, and now feeling she had to defend him, 'he said so. But—but his wife won't give him a divorce.'

Bella's hard look fixed on her sister. Reggie was three years younger than her in years, but so much younger in terms of experience of life. Her look softened as she questioned gently, 'You've told him "no", of course?'

Reggie's cheeks, pale till now, went pink. 'I—I couldn't.' And at her sister's sharp look, she said quickly, 'I didn't tell him "yes" either. It's—well, when I was with him it didn't seem such an awful thing to do. Clive made it sound the obvious solution. It was only when he'd dropped me off, when I was by myself, while I was getting over the shock—this is the first I knew he'd got a wife—and just now telling you about it, that it—that it began to feel all—all—well, not very nice somehow.'

'So you're actually going to give consideration to going to live with him?'

'I know it sounds awful. I know the grandparents would turn in their grave, but—but I love him. When I'm with him nothing else matters very much.' Even as she said it Reggie knew that it did matter. If she did go to live with Clive would she be able to take other people knowing about it? Word was bound to get out. Friends, people at work, they would all learn that she and Clive shared a flat, and that she was still Miss Barrington. Yet what was the alternative? She couldn't give him up.

'Tell me,' Bella asked, her look severe now after the way she had been, 'I know we've never discussed such intimate things before, but I don't think in the circumstances such a question is so far out of line—— Have you and Clive ever been to bed together?'

'No, of course not,' Reggie came back promptly.

'He's tried to get you there, of course?' Bella asked shrewdly, Reggie's high colour telling her the answer to that one. 'Then don't you see, love, that it just wouldn't be right for you? You were nine when we went to live with the grandparents, and they've instilled in you a lot of their values. Where at twelve I was already on the way to knowing what I wanted, starting to know for myself my own set of values, you were wide open. What I'm trying to say, love, is where such an arrangement might work for me, the inner you will find it difficult to live with your conscience during the times you're alone. And since you'll both be working, that will be often. I can't see you getting any happiness out of it.'

Bella might be right, Reggie was thinking as she lay awake hours later, nowhere near to making any sort of decision. Yet she loved Clive; had she not done so his suggestion might have sounded outrageous. But she hadn't been outraged. Perhaps she'd been in shock on hearing something so entirely different from what she had been expecting to hear, but looking back, she had felt no sense of outrage. Oh, if only sleep would come! That she had to be up for work in the morning didn't seem of prior importance. She wanted sleep more so, for a brief while anyway, it would stop the same thoughts from going around and around in her brain.

Her problem was still with her when she got out of bed the next morning. She looked across at Bella still sound asleep in the other bed, and, careful not to wake her, went quietly from the room. Bella didn't have to go to work. She had given up her dancing career when she had returned home suddenly from South America last month, and with her and James being married so soon it hadn't seemed worthwhile looking for anything in the meantime.

Funny thing that, she mused, leaving her own problems for the moment and avoiding her tired eyes in the mirror. James and Bella had had a blazing row when Bella had signed a contract that was to have kept her in South America up until some time in March. She had told her of his 'South America or me' ultimatum. But by then it was too late, her contract was signed, so Bella had gone. It just showed, though, how much she loved James, for within a month she was back, having somehow wriggled her way out of her contract. When James had heard she had done it for him he had straightaway popped the question, and not losing any time had put down a deposit on a house in Wellesbourne, a village near to Stratford-on-Avon where he worked as an architect.

Reggie and Clive had gone with them to the house one day. She and Clive had gone to Stratford afterwards. They had walked alongside the river . . .

Reggie brought her thoughts back abruptly. Clive was flying off to the States today. To be fair to her, he had said, he wouldn't write; he knew by now that she had some high principles and intended to leave her alone to come to her decision.

That Tuesday proved to be a long day. But eventually she was able to cover her typewriter and head her battered Mini, that was essential although it drained her resources, through the London suburbs.

Bella had gone to Wellesbourne today, to take some measurements, she said, an unneeded smoke-screen in her desire to snatch every moment she could with James, for the house couldn't need that much measuring, Reggie thought.

It had been an unusually warm day for December and had it been a summer's day, Reggie would have been wary of a thunderstorm. But whoever heard of thunder in December? And besides, she had too much else on her mind. Clive would be landing about now. She had hoped, for all he said he wouldn't, that he might ring, but he hadn't. Oh, how could she say no, she wouldn't go to live with him, when just to see him again would have her wanting to say yes?

Someone at her door bell had her going down to answer it. A mousy, neatly dressed woman about a couple of years older than herself stood there. She was studying her, making no attempt to state why she had called.

'What . . .?' Reggie began, only to find the stranger had at the same time found her tongue.

'Are you Regina Barrington?'

'Yes,' she agreed, puzzled why the woman should appear to sag at the word as though that confirmation defeated her.

'I just knew you'd be beautiful.'

Even more puzzled why her unknown visitor should pass comment on her blonde hair, blue eyes and passable features, Reggie thought it about time she found out what the woman wanted.

'I'm sorry,' she said, 'but I don't think I know you, do I?'

'Clive would hate it if he knew I was coming to see you,' said the woman, and just the mention of Clive's name had ominous warning signals flashing in Reggie's head, 'but I had to come. My name is Irene Walker—I'm Clive's wife.'

Reggie felt hot all over half an hour later when Irene Walker had left the apartment. It had very little to do with the warm evening, she thought, that her hands felt moist, or that her clothes felt as though they were sticking to her.

Never had she imagined herself in such a situation.

Never had she felt so embarrassed in her life. And yet, though her love for Clive was still unwavering, the shock of learning from Irene Walker that Clive had called to see her before going to the airport to once more ask her to divorce him, and her subsequent revelation that there were two children from the marriage, could not help but weaken the respect she had for him that he had not told her.

'Clive rang before breakfast this morning,' Irene Walker had told her. 'He said he was off to the States and wanted to come round before he went. He was just checking that I wouldn't be out and so saving himself from having a wasted journey. With him not being here for Christmas I thought he was coming to say cheerio to the children . . .'

'Children?' Reggie had gasped, her shock so evident, Irene Walker had immediately seen she had known nothing about them.

'He didn't tell you about them, did he?' she said slowly, then, 'But he's not ashamed of them. He takes them out every Saturday.'

This explanation of why she never saw Clive on Saturdays either went right over Reggie's head as she struggled against the news she had just heard.

'Tommy's six, Dawn is five,' Irene went on to inform her, when she could have done without knowing the children's names. Guilt was growing in her fast enough, for all she had been innocent of their existence, without their names endorsing the established fact that they were flesh and blood little human beings, a product of the love Clive and this woman must once have shared.

Too numbed at the news she had just received to say anything, she had listened while Irene told her that Clive's visit had not been primarily to tell the children that Daddy wouldn't be there to see them at Christmas—

the word 'Daddy' being another knife-thrust to Reggie—
but to again try and get her to agree to a divorce.

'I said no,' she carried on. 'Then Clive told me about
you. He said he wanted to marry you, that he loved
you . . .' Her voice broke, making it clear she still loved
her husband, causing a feeling something akin to shame
to wash over Reggie. Then Irene Walker had pulled herself together and was continuing, 'He wasn't very pleased
that I said no, but I refused to discuss it, so we then got
round to talking of other matters—money mainly,' she
added, without going into detail. 'The children's financial
security is important to me, so I asked what provision had
been made should he have an accident or anything while
abroad—these things can take ages to sort out and children's feet don't stop growing while insurances are being
settled.'

Every word she said about Clive's children, the fact
that they seemed constantly in need of new shoes, was a
hammer blow to Reggie; the only thing she could do was
hope to keep the emotion she was feeling from showing in
her face.

'Clive said he'd seen to all that, that I was still down as
his next of kin, and that his company would see we were
looked after. I think I must have got used to looking on
the black side,' Irene said, a selfconscious smile breaking
briefly on her sad mouth. 'Anyway, since Clive seemed to
think such a lot of you, I asked for your address in case
something dreadful happened to him—you read such terrible things in the paper, don't you?' she put in, not expecting a reply. 'I said to him that if he did have an
accident you would want to know straight away rather
than be kept in ignorance. I could see Clive would want
you to go to him in that event, so after some hesitation he
told me where you lived, though first making me promise
not to use it unless anything awful happened to him.'

'But you broke your promise,' said Reggie, not that it seemed all that important. More important was the fact that Clive had kept her in ignorance of his children.

'I didn't mean to, honestly I didn't. But I've had it on my mind all day about me refusing to consent to a divorce. Then I got to wondering if you were pregnant . . .'

'Pregnant!' The exclamation was out before she could hold it back.

'Forgive me,' said Irene, instantly apologetic, making Reggie feel more like a worm than ever that she should be apologising, to her! 'But I was carrying Tommy when Clive and I were married, so I couldn't help wondering, since he's so keen to marry you if the same . . . I don't want to divorce him, but if there was a child on the way—don't you see, I had to know.'

'I'm not pregnant,' Reggie had said woodenly, and there had seemed very little to say after that. Irene Walker had apologised once more for calling and a more than ever mixed up Reggie had gone with her to the outside door, to return to her flat with her mind not knowing where to start with this latest development.

She was definitely in no mood for tomfool telephone calls. The ringing of the phone greeted her as she went into the sitting room, and a sigh escaped as she picked up the phone and gave the number.

'Am I speaking with Regina Barrington?' asked a tough-sounding, foreign-accented voice.

'Yes, I'm Regina Barrington,' she said tonelessly, not twigging yet that one of Bella's theatrical friends was up to a practical joke.

'This is Severo Cardenosa,' the voice said, his tones hardening on hearing he was speaking with the party he wanted. There was a pause as though he expected the name to mean something to her.

'Yes,' she said, not having a clue who Severo Cardenosa was—and very few people ever called her Regina.

'Do not pretend you have forgotten me,' the voice said threateningly, 'or the bargain we made.'

'Bargain?' As she said the word light began to filter in. For Bella's sake she would have to play it through, but she felt more like crying than keeping her end up with one of Bella's nutty friends.

'You have been well paid for the part you are to play.' The voice was coldly angry now, earning full marks for top grade acting from Reggie, who had too much on her mind to want to participate. Then she found she didn't have to participate, for all the instructions were coming from the other end. 'It is most inconvenient for me to come to get you,' the voice said ominously, 'but make no mistake, Regina Barrington, unless you get here by the end of the week, then at some date in the very near future I shall come personally to collect you.'

Whether she would have answered anything to that, tried to play it along further, though the man was playing at being some horrible-sounding Severo Cardenosa up to the hilt—never had she heard such a threatening tone— she never discovered. For just then, without warning through where she had forgotten to draw the curtains, lightning forked in the sky, thunder cracked about her head and panic she despaired of ever losing in thunderstorms had her by the throat. The phone was back on its rest before she knew it, whether dropped from her hand or placed there she had no recollection. All she knew was that from somewhere she had to find the courage to go over to the windows and shut out that lightning.

Ten minutes later Bella burst into the room, her eyes straightway going to the settee where a white-faced Reggie sat with her fingers in her ears.

'Oh, love!' she exclaimed, going quickly over and

taking hold of her hands. 'I put my foot down as soon as it started to thunder.'

Reggie was relieved to see her and offered what she could in the way of a smile, her trembling body showing what she was going through.

'It will get better one of these days,' Bella tried to comfort her, knowing her sister's terrible fear stemmed from the day thirteen years ago when her parents had left her, their elder daughter, to stay with her grandparents and had driven away with young Reggie waving happily from the back window of the car. On their way they had run into a violent storm, and when lightning had bounced off the car it had aqua-planed on roads that were a river of water, coming to a standstill by crashing into a tree. Reggie had seen the broken, lifeless bodies of her parents just before she had lost consciousness. 'It's passing over,' she said, striving for a bracing note. 'Let's have a cup of tea.'

Loath to touch anything electrical, Reggie fought hard to get herself under control while Bella busied herself in the kitchen.

'How did your day go?' she asked when Bella returned with the tray, trying for normality but keeping a wary ear alert for thunder.

Bella's face took on a secretive smile. 'Lovely,' she said, almost purring, not attempting to cover the pleasure of her day by the pretence of measuring.

'You're back early.'

'We had thunder in Wellesbourne. My intuition told me it might be travelling this way.'

'Oh, Bella, you cut short your day for me! Didn't James mind?'

Briefly her sister frowned, then grinned, saying airily, 'Well, you know how possessive James is. He seems to want my complete and undivided attention at all times.

But as I told him, from Boxing Day onwards I shall devote all my time to him. Until then I have a little sister whom I soon won't be seeing so much of.'

Bella kept up bright chatter for another ten minutes as they sipped their tea. Reggie knew it was to keep her mind away from the thought that the thunderstorm, which had now departed, might yet return.

Having run out of amusing incidents, Bella ceased talking for the sake of talking, and suddenly asked, 'Did Clive ring before he went? I suspected you were hoping he might.'

'No.' Reggie felt no amazement that the thunderstorm had taken all remembrance of Clive and Irene Walker from her mind. Her fear of storms tended to freeze her thinking power. 'Clive didn't ring. But his wife called.'

'His wife!' Bella exclaimed, astonished. 'You mean she actually telephoned you!'

Reggie shook her head, 'She called in person,' and went on to relate, watching as her sister's mouth firmed into an unforgiving line, everything that had passed between her and Clive's wife, ending with a bruised, 'I can't think why he didn't say anything about the children last night.'

'I can,' said Bella promptly. 'He knew damn well any chance of you going to live with him when you knew about them would be right up the Swanee.'

She was right, of course. It would be bad enough even if she was able to take 'living the wrong side of the broom', as her horrified Gran would have put it, without having her conscience nagging at her, as she knew it would, that somehow she was depriving Clive's children of time they should have with their father. What happiness would there be for her then? And yet, as underhand as it might seem Clive had been, she still loved him.

Suddenly, without her being aware the decision had

been made, words were leaving her, the air upon them cementing the conviction of what she had to do.

'I'm going away, Bella,' she said.

'Away? Where? What are you talking about?'

'I've got to get away from London,' said Reggie, realising at last that it was the only course open to her. 'I've got to be where Clive can't find me when he returns.'

'You love him that much?'

'I feel strong now,' she explained. 'Able to pack up my job, give up this flat, try and make a new life for myself. But I have to do it before Clive comes back.'

'The weakness of love,' Bella put in thoughtfully. 'You think all your resolves will vanish the moment you see him again?'

'I—I just don't know,' Reggie answered hopelessly.

'It's not going to be easy for you,' Bella said gently, and Reggie knew she was referring to her own separation from James and how, after a month away from him in South America, the love she had for him had been stronger than all her independence and assertions before she went that no man was going to tell her what to do.

From then on it was Bella who became the more practical of the two. 'You can hand in your resignation at the office tomorrow,' she instructed. 'I'll see the landlord about the flat. You've got a couple of weekends in which to decide where you want to live and do something about finding accommodation.' She broke off, a thought suddenly occurring to her. 'Hey, why not come to Warwickshire? You might be able to find somewhere near to James and me. You're a good secretary, you shouldn't have any trouble getting a job in Stratford. You . . .'

Reggie stopped her right there, James' possessiveness uppermost in her mind. He liked her, she thought, as she liked him. But with James wanting Bella all to himself, he wouldn't take very kindly to having Reggie living on his doorstep.

'No,' she said. 'It wouldn't work,' and when Bella looked as though to argue why wouldn't it, she told her, 'Beside any other consideration, the first place Clive is going to start looking for me is with you.'

'I'd forgotten he'd been to the house in Wellesbourne.' Bella backed down, taking her point.

By the time they went to bed it had all been worked out that whether they liked it at the office or not tomorrow, Reggie was going to tell them she was leaving—for obscure family reasons, which they couldn't very well question—on Christmas Eve.

Yawning, Bella got into bed, freely admitting to being bushed, and Reggie was about to turn out the lamp on the low chest of drawers that separated the two beds when Bella asked casually:

'Nobody rang for me, I suppose?' She had a whole host of friends, but was gradually dropping out of circulation and wasn't too unhappy about the situation.

About to say 'No', Reggie remembered the oddball telephone call cut short by the thunderstorm. 'Only some nutty friend of yours rang asking for me—though why he asked for me I don't know, other than that he probably knew you'd rumble him straight away.'

'Nutty friend of mine?' Bella sounded intrigued as she propped herself up on an elbow. 'Well, they're not in short supply. Which one was it—any idea?'

Feeling slightly amused now where amusement had been far from her at the time, Reggie grinned, and was in no way prepared for the shock with which Bella received what she said next. It was startling.

'Not a clue. He adopted a fake foreign accent, called himself,' she paused, wanting to get it right, then brought out the name, 'Severo Cardenosa,' and felt her own colour drain as Bella went ashen.

'Severo Cardenosa!' The horrified expression on her sister's face as she repeated the name, without her loss of colour, was enough to have Reggie leaping out of bed and going to her.

'There is such a person?' she questioned urgently, fast coming away from being the little sister who looked to Bella for guidance, and suddenly taking charge as Bella buried her head in her hands and rocked as she cried:

'Oh, my God—oh, my God! Severo Cardenosa has the power to ruin my life!'

CHAPTER TWO

'Ruin your life?' Reggie echoed, her mind darting all ways in the face of her sister's distress, but coming up with nothing other than that the dark threatening tones she had heard in that coldly angry voice had been for real. It hadn't been the joke she had assumed it to be!

'Who is he?' she asked quickly when it looked as though Bella wasn't going to come out of her state of near collapse. 'What's it all about, Bella?'

Her face still ashen, Bella raised her head from her hands. 'I met him in Uruguay.'

'He's a South American?'

She nodded. 'I never for a moment thought he'd find me once I'd left the country. He's got loads of charm once he cares to use it, I'll bet one of the girls gave him my address and phone number.'

'But why should he come looking for you? And is it Uruguay he wants you to go to before the end of the week?' It all sounded crazy to Reggie, but before she could say as much, Bella was rapidly firing the question:

'Is that what he said? That he wants me to go there?'

'He said if you didn't, though it was inconvenient at

the moment, to make no mistake, he would come to collect you.'

'Oh no!' Bella groaned, if possible looking whiter than ever. Then, urgently, 'Tell me word for word what he said.'

Trying to remember everything, Reggie repeated as much as she could recall, and in doing so remembered something she had forgotten since Bella's transition from a happy young woman to the frightened person she looked at the moment.

'What did he mean by "You've been paid for the part you're to play"? And why on earth did he use my name? I might have got a word wrong here and there, but he definitely said, "Make no mistake, Regina Barrington . . ."'

She stopped speaking as everything she had repeated became too much for Bella, who suddenly burst into tears. Unable to remember the last time she had seen her cry, she was appalled and in a moment had her arms around her.

'You'd better tell me everything,' she said gently, and, winningly, 'It can't be as bad as all that.'

'Oh yes, it can,' sobbed Bella.

Reggie's mind was most definitely not on her work the next day. Her own problems, her need to leave London before Clive returned, had to take a back seat. Though since it was still her intention to put herself out of his orbit, she did remember to type out her resignation. Mr Elford, her boss, was not too pleased that she was leaving at such short notice, but with so much else on her mind, Bella's revelations having shaken her rigid, his sulky manner with her for the rest of the morning was the lesser of her worries.

At lunch time she took herself off to a park bench and

wondered yet again how Bella could have done such a thing. No wonder she was scared stiff! If James ever found out, aside from his possessive manner, that upstanding, no-nonsense streak in him would put an end to all their plans to marry.

It was so out of character for Bella to have done what she had, so against the way they had both been brought up. Yet there was no disbelieving it. From Bella's own lips Reggie had heard that not only had she broken her contract to stay with the dance troupe until the end of the South American summer, but the worst part of all was that she had made a contract with Severo Cardenosa, unwritten though it might be a contract none the less, and had broken that contract too. No wonder he had been angry!

Astonished, unable to credit what she was hearing, she had questioned Bella, and was still having difficulty in believing what she had heard.

Her sister had been visiting one of the girls who, because she had been involved in a motor accident in Montevideo, had been taken to hospital there, not to the glamorous resort of Punta del Este some eighty or so miles away where they were working.

Bella admitted she had been miles away as she neared the hospital, her thoughts with James, anger at his bossy ultimatum pulling against a longing to be with him, when turning a corner she had literally been knocked off her feet by a man with his mind on his own problems.

'He helped me up,' Bella had told her, 'and I suppose I must have been looking a little winded, because he straight away offered to take me for refreshment. At first I thought he was just trying his luck—that was until I realised when he didn't follow through that he was just expressing the courtesy that's common to all Uruguayans.'

'So you went with him?'

'Normally I wouldn't have done, I'd already got my breath back, but there was something about this Severo Cardenosa I found intriguing. It wasn't until we were sitting drinking tea that I realised what it was.'

'He was good-looking?'

'He's that all right. But it wasn't his looks that had me going with him, so much as the fact he didn't appear to notice me as a woman. Oh, I'm sure he'd already registered that I had everything in the right place—he's very much a man in that direction, of that I'm certain. But, apart from his obeying all the politeness of his nationality, his eyes didn't make a meal of me as I'm used to happening.'

Reggie accepted that as fair comment. Bella was beautiful, in ways as well as manner, it was only natural for men to want to stare at her.

'Well, it piqued me to find that though he was observing all the niceties of such an occasion he just wasn't seeing me, so without really thinking too much about it I decided to try my hand at seeing how long it would take me to thaw him out.'

'You *were* piqued, weren't you?'

'I'm not used to being ignored,' Bella responded, her voice taking a slight edge.

'Of course you're not,' Reggie agreed honestly.

Bella's face softened before she continued. 'Anyway, to get him talking I told him I was staying at Punta del Este, not mentioning that I was a dancer because if he did start to breathe heavily then I would have achieved what I wanted and I intended to duck out.'

Reggie felt slight shock on learning that Bella had a man-teasing streak in her, but she loved her too much to think of it as something she shouldn't possess. 'How long did it take you—to get the heavy breathing, I mean?' she asked, covering her surprise.

'I didn't. To be courteous, he in turn told me he came from the interior, and then he asked if I was enjoying my holiday. Then he enquired if I would like more tea. It seemed to me then that he was impatient to be away, for all he was covering it with politeness, and for my sins I let it niggle me that he was barely seeing me. I was determined then that he would see me as a young and attractive female. So I said I was rather thirsty, telling him the shock of cannoning into him must have lowered my sugar content. He couldn't do any other then than order more tea, which I took my time about drinking while I got in there with all the leading questions.'

'Leading questions?' Reggie queried, not sure what she meant.

'Was he married—that sort of thing. No, he told me briefly, looking at his watch to give me the hint. He seemed to go away from me as I asked if he'd got a steady girl-friend and answered, almost absently, I thought, "No", and appeared to forget I was there as he added, "Right at this moment, would that I had". Well, that puzzled me, because he'd got everything it takes and then some. But I could see from his face that he was on the point of being torn between the politeness of his race and the urge that was in him to tell me to go to the devil.'

'Perhaps he had an urgent appointment,' Reggie suggested.

'It wasn't all that urgent, but when he said, "You appear to have recovered from your fall. Would you excuse me, I am anxious to visit a relative in hospital," I realised he must think a lot of this relative and that while ten or so minutes with me wouldn't change anything, he was eager to find out how his relation was. "I'm visiting the hospital too," I told him as he settled the bill. Since we were both visiting the same hospital it would have been daft not to walk together.'

Reggie had thought Bella had lost some of her own anxiety as, talking compulsively, the shock she had received loosening her tongue, she told her of her meeting with Severo Cardenosa in Montevideo. But suddenly that desperate look was back as she went on with her story.

'Oh, if only my stupid vanity hadn't been pricked because I'd met one man who didn't fancy me,' she cried. 'We could so easily have parted at the hospital. But no, I couldn't leave well enough alone. I found out as we walked along that it was his grandfather he was visiting. And with a flash of insight one sometimes gets I was suddenly positive his remark about wishing he had a steady girl-friend was something to do with the old man—so I asked him.'

'You didn't!' For the first time Reggie thought her sister had gone too far.

'I couldn't see any reason why I shouldn't. Though I didn't think he was going to answer, but with his mind more on his grandfather than me—Uruguayans have a strong sense of family—he revealed that the old chap was very ill and was fretting that he was going to die before he saw his grandson married.'

'So that's what he meant,' said Reggie, her brain active. 'Had he a steady girl-friend, been intending to get married, his grandfather would die happy.'

'Exactly what I thought. I'm not as sentimental as you, I admit, but I couldn't help thinking of our dear grandparents. So off the top of my head I offered to go with him to visit his grandfather as his steady.'

That was just typical of the kindly action Bella would take, Reggie thought, her heart warming to her for her goodness. Though things must have gone badly wrong for her to get into the state she had on learning that Severo Cardenosa had traced her to England.

'He took you up on your offer?' she asked.

'Not straight away. He stopped dead, and a more suspicious look I never encountered. It was obvious he was wondering what I hoped to get out of it.'

'Some people!' Reggie interjected with feeling.

'He then led me to a seat and I could tell he was weighing up the idea. Then he must have decided that whatever I was after it would be worth it to send the old man on his way happy.'

'He accepted your offer?'

Bella nodded. 'He seemed to like the idea the more we talked about it, telling me his grandfather had married an English girl and would be over the moon to think he would be doing the same. But when he told me his name and asked mine—well, it was then that I began to have second thoughts.'

'You told him you'd changed your mind?'

'No, no, I couldn't. I would have felt too much of a fool. James had been out of my mind for some time, but with Severo asking my name, looking so well-to-do, I had terrifying visions of an announcement of my engagement to him appearing in *La Mañana*, of it getting into the English press if our publicist was doing his stuff, I wouldn't have stood a chance of getting back with James if that happened—you know how stuffy he can be sometimes.'

'So you didn't give him your own name?' The fog was clearing.

'I was getting panicky, he was waiting to hear who I was, and yours was the only name I could think of besides my own. Rosabel Barrington and my stage name Bella Lawson are both names James knows me by.'

'So you told this Severo Cardenosa you were Regina Barrington.'

'I knew you wouldn't mind under the circumstances,' said Bella, not giving Reggie the chance to discover whether she would or not as she went on, 'Anyway, I went with him to see the old man. He looked dreadfully ill, but gripped on to my hand as though I was his long-lost granddaughter when Severo introduced me.'

'Did you see the old man again?' Reggie questioned, wondering, in all she had heard, why it should appear to Bella that she would be in such terrible trouble if Severo Cardenosa came to get her as he had said he would. Surely James would understand the warmth in her to have done what she so impulsively had?

'No—I didn't see him again,' Bella said slowly. 'I realised by the time the visit was over that I was running short of time and I decided to visit the girl who'd taken me to the hospital in the first place another day. Severo came out of the hospital with me, saying he was committed to see another relative who was staying in a hotel in Montevideo and couldn't drive me back to Punta del Este. Though he did insist on getting me a taxi and settling the fare before I left. That in itself told me he wasn't short of a copper or two.'

'But *why* is this Severo Cardenosa coming after you? He sounded as though he meant every word on the phone. Had I realised it wasn't one of your idiot friends I would have been terrified.' Reggie only just managed to suppress a shudder at the remembrance of that hard voice as Bella's face again whitened. 'Oh, Bella, tell me—and what the heck did he mean by you having been well paid for the part you had to play?'

A couple of quarrelsome birds fighting over a bread crust someone had thrown down brought her round to the fact that if she didn't get her skates on she was going to be late getting back to the office, something not guaranteed to improve Mr Elford's sulks any.

But during the afternoon, the matter in her typewriter not being anything requiring her full attention, her mind returned again to Bella and the mess she had got herself into. Had she been in touch with Severo Cardenosa yet? She had said she was going to try ringing him today, though since he was the owner of a cattle ranch, he could well be out with his stock.

Again she wondered how Bella could have done such a thing! For she had been rocked to her very foundations when Bella had gone on to reveal that the 'You have been well paid' Severo Cardenosa had spoken of, the bargain he had referred to, was that in return for her going on with the pretence that she was his fiancée, he had paid her *ten thousand pounds!*

That Bella had not only *taken* his money but then gone back on her word had shattered her; anything after that was not nearly so earth-shaking. Though how Bella could have told James she had inherited some money and used that money for the deposit on the house when there had been a hold-up on James' own money coming through— his money being spent on furnishings when it arrived a week later—Reggie just couldn't fathom.

No wonder Bella had been panic-stricken! Love her he might, but if James heard a word of this he would never stand for it—he must never be allowed to find out.

Constantly she thought about what Bella had told her, examining, re-examining, trying to find some way of saving her sister's future. There was no doubt Bella was in love with James—so much in love that she had last night declared with an intensity that alarmed her that if she couldn't have James then life wasn't worth living.

Terrified that her sister was having thoughts of doing away with herself, Reggie had told her there must be some way out, that she could count on her to do anything at all no matter how small or how big to help her. She had been the one to urge Bella to get in touch with this Severo. Pray God his attitude had softened from what it had been last night.

Not that she held out much hopes for that; he sounded a tough character. Reggie began searching for some way out, going over again the remainder of what Bella had told her. James had again been occupying most of her thoughts three days later, her little exploit in Montevideo on the way to being forgotten, when coming out of her hotel she had met Severo Cardenosa coming in. He had remembered the name of the hotel she had given to the taxi driver and had come looking for her. Intrigued, she had gone with him to have coffee, where he had explained that although his grandfather's life expectancy was not long, amazingly, since meeting her and believing his grandson was shortly to put his bachelorhood behind him—was marrying an English girl the way he had—the old man had taken on a new lease of life, and was improving daily. There was even talk of him leaving hospital. Severo had then come to the purpose of his coming to Punta del Este, telling Bella that though physically weak his grandfather had all his mental faculties, causing Severo to be very concerned that he would soon realise, when no English fiancée appeared at the *estancia*, that it had been a put-up job, the result of which could cause an immediate relapse from which he would not recover. He had then put to Bella the most surprising proposition that she should go and stay at the *estancia* for the remainder of his grandfather's life.

'From the way he was talking it sounded as though the old chap hadn't got very long to go anyway,' Bella had said, and then she said something that had Reggie's eyes growing wide that she seemed to have grown a mercenary streak in her make-up. 'Well, I was still anti-James more times than I was pro-James, so I told Severo that I stood to lose a great deal of money if I agreed to do as he asked, that I was a dancer, and apart from the money, since what he was asking would mean I should have to break my contract, I would find it very difficult to get back into dancing again.'

Bella talking about money when Severo Cardenosa must have been a very worried man, even if he was as horrible as the tone of his voice suggested, had Reggie feeling embarrassed on her behalf, but she swallowed it down, asking:

'What did he say to that?'

'Gave me a hard look I didn't care much for, just as though he thought I was out for all I could get, and then went all arrogant and proud and told me that naturally he didn't intend I should be out of pocket and suggested a figure of ten thousand pounds sterling.'

And while Reggie had gasped in astonishment Bella had gone on to say she had agreed to his proposal, whereupon he had given her his cheque, instructing her that since he was commuting from his home to Montevideo frequently and was unsure what his exact movements were going to be, she should the following week take a plane to the airport at Durazno where he would be sure to meet her.

'What went wrong?' Reggie asked quietly, for clearly something had.

'Nothing went wrong,' said Bella, 'except that when I went to catch the flight to Durazno I was so overwhelmed by a compulsion to see James—it was all I could think about—I flew home instead.'

Mr Elford did not even bother to say goodnight as Reggie left the office that night, letting her know she wasn't in for a very rosy time and that when Christmas Eve did arrive she would be heartily glad. Though with everything piling up, not least the mental torture she was suffering over Clive, if Mr Elford decided to play sulky schoolboy from now till then she doubted it would bother her all that much.

As she let herself into the flat, there was hope in her heart that Bella had found Severo Cardenosa in a more amiable frame of mind. But after one look at her sister's pale, ravaged face, her red eyes showing she had been indulging in another bout of weeping, that hope faded.

'What did he say?' she asked, no need for preamble.

'Not a lot,' said Bella listlessly. 'But what he did say was short and to the point. Grandfather is now out of hospital and I've got three choices—I go, he comes, or he wants his money back. He's no fool, he knows I would have spent it by now.'

Reggie perched herself on the settee beside her. It was hopeless, hopeless. 'Want some tea?' she enquired.

'No, thanks.'

Sombrely the two girls sat, both looking into space as though hoping some bright idea would show itself. Unconsciously Reggie sighed.

'I'm sorry to burden you with my problem—you've got enough of your own, haven't you, chick?' Bella, hearing her sigh, said regretfully. 'Poor Reggie,' she said, thinking to add, 'Did you give your notice in today?'

Reggie nodded. 'Received with displeasure.'

'It's the only thing to do. Get right away from Clive. Make a fresh . . .' Bella stopped, the sound of her sharply sucked in breath having Reggie's head turning to look at her.

Bella's face was suddenly animated, the first sign of life she had seen in her since she had got into bed last night.

'What is it?' she asked, knowing her sister had just thought of something.

'I've just had a great idea,' Bella beamed, almost laughing her relief was so immense. 'Oh, Reggie, what a dumbo I've been! Sitting here all day going demented trying to find a way out when the way out has been obvious all along!'

'Well, don't keep it to yourself.' Her own heart lifted to see Bella looking happy again. 'What have you just thought of?' Eagerly she waited for Bella to tell her. But when she did she felt near to fainting with shock.

'You're upping sticks because you're afraid you won't have the strength to say no to Clive. You're looking for somewhere to go where Clive won't find you when he comes back. He'll never think of looking for you in South America.'

'South America!'

'Why, oh, why didn't I think of it before?' said Bella, if she had heard her sister's startled exclamation taking no heed. 'It's perfect—perfect! You get to be where Clive can't get to you. Severo Cardenosa gets a fiancée by the name of Regina Barrington, and I,' her voice softened, 'and I get James.'

Suddenly Bella was hungry. Reggie's appetite had gone altogether as her protests were walked over. 'Come on, let's see what there is to eat.'

Over pork chops and vegetables, Reggie tried to get Bella to see what a nonsense her idea was. 'Severo Cardenosa will never go for it,' she protested.

'Why shouldn't he?' Bella demanded to know. 'His grandfather thinks he's engaged to an English girl called Regina Barrington. You're English, aren't you, and your name is Regina Barrington.'

'Yes, but . . .' She tried again, a dreadful feeling coming over her that Bella was so taken with her idea she was going to refuse to listen to all reason.

'If you're going to say that Grandfather Cardenosa has seen me then that needn't bother you. We both have blonde hair and he had his eyes closed most of the time, just lay there holding my hand. Besides which,' she asserted sweepingly, 'all old men over eighty wear glasses, and he didn't have his specs on at the time.'

Feeling she was being bulldozed along, Reggie tried again. 'But Severo Car . . .'

'You've no need to worry about him. Provided an English fiancée turns up looking something like me,' Bella paused to examine Reggie's features, seeing suddenly for the first time that although there were similarities between them, Reggie was beautiful in a different, more lasting way. 'Do you know, you're quite something, young Reggie—Severo Cardenosa would have to be less of a man than I'm sure he is not to welcome you with open arms.'

'Open arms!' Reggie's heart began to thump, unsure whether it was from the fright of what was taking place, or the idea of being in the arms of that man who was threatening to ruin Bella's life if something wasn't done about it.

'Don't look so petrified. Nothing like what you're thinking went on between him and me. I told you this whole mess started in the first place because he didn't fancy me, and it showed. You've got nothing to worry about in that direction, I promise you. All Severo wants is a platonic fiancée until such time—probably fairly soon now—as the old man dies.'

Reggie's heart steadied down with Bella's promise. That was until she realised she was actually going along with her idea.

'I can't do it, Bella,' she said promptly. 'I . . .' The look of happiness vanishing from Bella's face had her protest floundering.

'Reggie—Reggie love,' Bella said coaxingly, 'would I let you go out there if I thought for one moment that the least possible harm would come to you?'

Reggie considered the question. 'No, you wouldn't,' she admitted, the feeling gathering momentum that she was in up above her head.

'And didn't you say only last night that if there was anything you could do, no matter how small or how big, you would do it?' Reggie nodded, her throat dry. Bella smiled, then said gently, 'And you do want to put as much distance possible between you and Clive, don't you?'

She wasn't sure any more. But because of all she'd said on the subject, she answered quietly, 'Yes.'

'There you are, then,' said Bella, and was off again, thoroughly enamoured of the idea. 'You speak Spanish too, so that will be a great asset, for all Severo speaks English like . . .'

'I don't speak Spanish,' Reggie put in, Bella's frowning look telling her she considered she was trying to be difficult. 'I know a bit of Spanish,' she said, knowing she was weak in trying to take that frown away, 'but if you remember, I dropped Spanish to concentrate on my French "O" level.'

'Well, you know enough to get by on, which is more than I did,' said Bella, and went on with making plans for her sister's departure before the end of the week.

'Wait a minute,' Reggie stopped her. 'I can't go that soon. Apart from Mr Elford already thinking I've got a cheek not giving him a full month's notice, I can't leave work before Christmas Eve, besides the masses I'll have to do here first.'

'But Severo wants a fiancée there by the end of this week,' Bella persuaded.

Having the uncomfortable feeling she had been press-ganged, her love for her sister being put to a very real test, Reggie found enough iron in her soul to resist her coaxing, her assurances that she would do everything there was to be done.

'No,' she said firmly. 'I haven't even got so much as a passport yet, plus the fact I shall have to sell the Mini to pay my air fair.'

'Severo will willingly pay that,' Bella asserted, only to read from Reggie's proud look that she would swim first.

'You'll have to ring him anyway to tell him a replacement fiancée is coming,' Reggie said reasonably. 'You can tell him, then, that—that I'm having passport difficulties because of the Christmas rush or something and that we'll let him know as soon as the arrangements are made this end.'

There was silence in the room for a few moments, the sisters each busy with their own thoughts, then Bella was saying, 'I shall have to ring him tomorrow. He—er—mentioned on the phone that I'd just caught him on his way out to catch a plane.'

The next evening Reggie, while half wishing Severo Cardenosa had turned the substitute offer down, and guiltily wondering how she could be so mean to have such a wish when her sister's happiness was at stake, asked her if she had been in touch with him.

Bella's back was to her as she answered, 'Yes, I rang him. He's gone for it.'

'Hmph,' Reggie grunted. 'Was he mad that you're not going?'

'Not a bit,' Bella said, turning to smile brightly. 'He's looking forward to meeting you.'

CHAPTER THREE

LOOKING forward to meeting her! It looked like it, Reggie thought some three weeks later. For three days now she had been cooling her heels in Montevideo, and still no sign of him.

He might not like it that it had been the first of January before she had left London—what a start to a new year!—but she couldn't help that her Mini had been difficult to sell. As it was, what she had got for it just about covered her air fare with very little left over.

It didn't take a mathematical genius to work out she wasn't going to be able to pay her hotel bill, and the longer Severo Cardenosa took in coming for her the more her feelings of trepidation were turning to anger.

Had it been left to her she would have booked into a more modest establishment, always supposing she could have got in somewhere at the peak of the summer season. But it hadn't been left to her. Severo had phoned the flat while she had been at work telling Bella, since he still apparently wasn't sure of his movements, he would book her into a hotel where she was to wait until he collected her.

That she had had gigantic misgivings about coming in the first place weren't helped any to hear she was to 'wait to be collected'. She felt even bigger misgivings having now abandoned her idea that at the most she would be spending only one night in the hotel, that she appeared to be a parcel sent for on impulse but was now a parcel any old time would do to pick up.

Her churned-up feelings were further aggravated that determined as she had been after that first night spent in the hotel not to telephone to remind him she was here, after two more nights spent in sleepless worrying, her resolve was weakening.

A mood of rebellion hit her when the time for dinner approached and her stomach complained that she had eaten only sparsely that day. Why shouldn't she go down to dinner? Her room was luxurious in every detail, but so what if it did face the Rambla—the miles long river-front drive. What if her room did have a splendid view of Montevideo Bay? If Severo Cardenosa thought she was going to stay stuck in her room waiting until he deigned to collect her, then he could think again!

Downstairs in the restaurant she felt better for having

eaten, but her short burst of rebellion hadn't lasted, and anxiety again set in that she looked like being stranded. Her imagination took flight. Bella would be petrified if she saw the headlines in the paper 'British girl stranded—deserted by Uruguayan fiancé'. She blinked, grinned at her fantasising and felt all loving to Bella as she recalled how beautiful she had looked on her wedding day.

Her face sobered as she left the restaurant, the plight she was in coming back to haunt her. She wouldn't ring him, though, she wouldn't, she determined. But as she neared the reception desk, the girl receptionist sent her a charming smile, and her footsteps faltered.

'Er—is it possible for me to send a telegram?'

The enquiry had left her without her realising she had the words formed, but when the receptionist answered, 'Certainly, madam. I will see that it goes straight away,' she suddenly thought, why not? She wouldn't actually be speaking to that cold voice, would she?

It took some minutes to decide what to put. If there was just the recipient of the telegram to consider, there would have been no problem. 'I'm here, where are you?' would have suited very nicely. But supposing Grandfather Cardenosa was about when her telegram was delivered?

It was as she finally wrote out what she had decided to send that the extent of her commitment in this venture hit her. If she passed this slip of paper over to the receptionist then she was really in at the deep end. There would be no going back. Severo would have to come for her—or have to make some very good excuse for ignoring her wire. For Bella's sake she would have to stay and play the loving fiancée until the old man died.

She pushed her message across the desk. Oh, what a mess—and it just wasn't in her to hope the old man wouldn't take too long in departing.

'To where shall I send it?'

The receptionist's natural enquiry had Reggie apologising and rooting in her bag for the address Bella had given her. 'Señor Severo Cardenosa, Estancia de Cardenosa, Cerros de Cielo,' she said, pausing while the receptionist's fingers caught up, rather proud of her accent, but glad the girl could speak English for all that, as she savoured the name Cerros de Cielo, doubting that it would be anywhere as lovely as it sounded, or as she had translated it, 'Hills of Paradise'. The receptionist looked up. 'Durazno,' Reggie completed.

Not until the next morning, still worried and having slept little better than the previous night, did she wonder if she should have worded her telegram a shade more formally. But by the time she was having breakfast rebellion was again with her. Oh, what the hell! If he didn't care for her, 'Can't wait to see you, darling' then that was his bad luck.

Though tempered with an uneasy feeling she was never going to see Severo Cardenosa, that he might not so much as stir himself to pick up a telephone, her mood of rebellion took a firmer hold than it had last night. She wasn't sitting in that room upstairs just waiting on the offchance that he would ring, that was for sure. She was at the reception desk before she could change her mind.

'I have to go out,' she told a fresh receptionist. 'My—fianceé may telephone. Would you take a message for me?'

Hardly knowing why she had bothered, Reggie walked briskly away from the desk, leaving the cooling air-conditioning of the hotel and going out into Montevideo's sun-drenched streets. To date she had made only small excursions from her hotel, but today she was in no hurry to return.

In the Plaza Independcia she stood for an age admiring the superb bronze statue of national hero José Gervasio Artigas on horseback, and from the Plaza Indepencia, too well aware of the thinness of her purse, she windowshopped her way along the Avenido 18 de Julio to the Plaza Cagancha, veering left along the wide Avenido 18 de Julio once more, an avenue commemorating the date in 1830 when Uruguay's constitution was proclaimed.

Since she had no intention of returning to her hotel until well into the afternoon—let Severo Cardenosa do a spot of waiting for her for a change, always supposing he had come down from his lofty high horse and bothered to telephone at all!—it was not yet midday when anxiety began to gnaw into rebellion and she started to grow fidgety to learn if he had left some message.

Walking quickly, she crossed the wide avenue, rebellion gone as she thought to try a short cut to get to the hotel the sooner. Her mind fully preoccupied, it came as something of a shock when raising her eyes she saw the one statue of all others she had heard about that she definitely had no interest in. Her footsteps faltered, panic fluttering up from nowhere to find herself face to face with Zorrillo de San Martin's famous statue of the Gaucho.

Fear was the only emotion she felt capable of as she looked back at the threatening gaucho. She forced her eyes away and began to hurry on, fear fading as she berated herself for the panic that had taken from her the awareness to appreciate the beauty of the sculpture. How ridiculous to feel so threatened by that dashing figure! As if it could harm her!

Reggie could have done without that inner voice that plagued while she scoffed at her imaginings that a bronze statue could make her feel so threatened, the inner voice that said—yes, but you haven't met the real thing yet, have you?

Nor likely to, the way things are going, she thought, as she reached her hotel. Severo Cardenosa was in no hurry to show himself. If she hadn't once heard his voice, seen how terrified Bella had been, she would now be wondering if he existed at all.

Because reception seemed to have an influx of people with enquiries, she decided to leave her own enquiry of was there any message for her until after she had been up to her room and rinsed her face and hands. Taking the lift, she was soon inserting her key in her door.

And then all thought of the nice refreshing wash she was going to have vanished, and shrieking alarm drove all thought from her mind. For her room was not un-occupied as she had every reason to believe it would be.

There in a chair he had obviously turned to face the door, long legs stretched out in front of him, his lean body at ease—at variance with the shrewd look in the most startling brilliant blue eyes fixed on her, startling especi-ally because the rest of him, bronze skin that covered a straight nose, firm mouth and square chin, was de-finitely of Uruguayan descent—sat a man whose looks, combined with the steady stare he was affording her, had the fear she had experienced when looking at the statue earlier come screaming to life.

How she didn't actually scream Reggie didn't know. Afterwards she awarded herself full marks for the way her voice sounded cool and fully composed, as she asked:

'Might I enquire exactly what you think you're doing in my room?'

For a moment she thought he wasn't going to answer, that he couldn't understand a word of English. She noticed then an alertness in him she had at first missed, then found that given he had a slight accent, he was as much at home in her language as she was.

'Your room?' he questioned. 'You are the sole occupant?'

Before her reply left her the suspicion was shrieking in her that Severo Cardenosa might not have bothered to telephone. He might well have come in person to answer her telegram—this could well be him!

'Yes,' she answered, praying with all her might that her air of calm wouldn't desert her now. Bella had said he was good-looking. He was that all right. But Bella hadn't said anything about those brilliantly blue eyes that took you apart and summed you up in ten seconds flat.

'Then, *señorita*,' his voice had been quiet up until this point, but as it toughened, became cold and hard like she had heard it on the telephone, Reggie knew no doubt about his identity, 'perhaps you wouldn't mind telling me who the *hell* you are?'

'My—friends call me Reggie,' she said, reminding herself that they were supposed to convince other people they were engaged and trying for a friendliness she didn't feel in the face of the aggression emanating from him. It was clear when he didn't reply that he favoured a more formal introduction, which left her gathering what cool she had left as she set about doing the thing properly. 'My name is Regina Barrington,' she amended, sure he knew anyway, and sailing on a brief moment of courage went on with flags flying, 'You, I presume, are Severo Cardenosa, my temporary fiancé.'

Without a word, Severo Cardenosa raised himself from his chair. Never once taking his eyes from her, he walked round to the side of her, his look going deliberately from her blonde hair all the way down, taking his time at various contours, to end at her sandalled feet.

Reggie was half way to crumpling before he had finished his inspection. But when next he spoke, if what he said had been purposely designed to take the wind out of her sails, then he couldn't have managed it better.

'So,' he said, his eyes going to her long silky hair, 'the bottle blonde has been substituted for the real thing. Tell me, *darling*, since you couldn't wait to see me—do I get a kiss of greeting?'

'It's not that sort of engagement and you know it,' she found enough energy to retort, knowing she was going through the worst five minutes she was ever likely to spend. 'I only worded my message like that in case you wanted to show it to your grandfather.'

At the word 'grandfather' a change came over him. If he had been trying to get a rise out of her for the sheer hell of it, then she judged her reminding him of why she was here put an end to all that.

'Your passport,' he commanded after a moment when it appeared his mind wasn't on her.

'My passport?'

'I wish to see it.'

Reggie rummaged in her bag, wanting to hit him over the head with it as she handed it over. Clearly he was saying he trusted neither of the Barrington sisters, and wanted to see for himself that she was who she said she was. A feeling of awkwardness, of shame, that because of what Bella had done her own word was being questioned beset her, kept her quiet as he checked the photograph that looked as if the photographer had had an off day, and read through her particulars.

'So, Regina Barrington, secretary, aged twenty-two,' he said, 'you have come to see what is in it for you, have you?'

'What's in it for me?' she gasped.

'You are saying you are not here on the—treasure trail?'

Never had any man made her so instantly hopping mad. 'No, I am not!' she retorted heatedly. She had always thought a girl who resorted to slapping a man's face showed a shocking lack of self-control, but for the first time in her life she found herself fighting hard to quell the impulse. She settled for going for him verbally instead. 'You know damn well why I'm here! If it wasn't for Bella . . .'

'Bella is a relation?' He chopped her off smartly. 'You both have the same surname.'

'She's my sister, as you well know,' Reggie spat at him.

Slowly Severo Cardenosa shook his head from side to side, succeeding without words in taking the stuffing out of her as he denied any such knowledge. Knocked sideways, all the heat went from her as she stared at him in shock and disbelief.

'You must know! Bella telephoned you to say I was coming in her place.' Her voice began to peter out as again he gave her that slow shake of his head. 'You told her,' she struggled on, 'that you were looking forward to meeting me.'

'Could it be your—sister lied to you?' he mocked, for all the world as though he didn't doubt Bella would lie her head off if it suited her, and conveying at the same time he thought Reggie was tarred with the same brush.

'Bella wouldn't lie to me,' Reggie stated, sounding nowhere near as positive as she would like to be, the awful truth dawning that since she could see no good reason why the man watching her so sardonically should lie, then her sister must have done. But even while she was trying to come to terms with that staggering fact, Severo Cardenosa had dropped his mocking air and was bitingly accusing her.

'Your sister told you everything that had taken place. Between you you dreamed up this little scheme of trying to take me for another ten thousand. Isn't that the truth?' he demanded, having apparently come to the conclusion that both sisters were out for all they could get.

'No, it isn't!' she flashed, her right hand itching to meet his taut cheek.

His look said he didn't believe her, without his infuriating challenge of, 'Why then are you here in her place?'

Too angry at the nerve of him to suggest she would touch a penny of his money, she spoke on a tide of temper that ignored the need for caution.

'Bella became Mrs James Usher on Boxing Day.' Sarcasm came to help her out. 'I don't think her husband would take very kindly to her carrying out this assignment, do you?'

Sarcasm got her nowhere. But the sneering way he said, 'Her husband is in this too, is he?' had her anger going over the top.

She'd waited four days for this! Four days of fretting and worrying, and what had she got at the end of it?— nothing but a discovery that unbelievably Bella had lied to her, and that this—this swine of a man thought she was no better than a cheap gold-digger here to see what was in it for her.

'No,' she exploded, 'James doesn't know. He'd be absolutely horrified if he knew what Bella had done. As I was myself,' she added hotly, her deeply blue eyes flashing that he seemed impervious to her anger and nowhere near on the way to believing her. 'I took the first phone call from you—I thought it was a joke until Bella came home and said it wasn't. I didn't want to come here— and now that I've met you I wish I hadn't!'

He remained unimpressed, offering a sarcastic, 'So you have decided to take the next plane home?'

The swine! If only she could. Suddenly the terrible position she was in swamped her. She would be hard put to it to find the fare as far as Rio. Obviously Severo Cardenosa had taken one look and taken a violent dislike to her, a dislike that was so great that even the threat of a setback to his grandfather's health wouldn't have him taking her on as a substitute for Bella. Anger left her, defeat nullifying it. Never more had she wanted to be safely home in England, safe with Clive. Tears sprang to her eyes, choking her throat, making her voice husky as she clung to what pride she could find and said with quiet dignity:

'I apologise for what Bella has done. My only purpose in coming was to settle my sister's debt.' He was so still, it unnerved her; she couldn't look at him any longer, so she moved past him to stare unseeingly at the Bay. 'I'm sorry too, that you don't find me a suitable substitute . . .'

Suddenly panicky thoughts of what on earth was she going to do now were pushed to the background as alarm at the weapon she had handed him to ruin Bella's happiness seized her. Oh, why had she lost her temper, told him Bella was married, how appalled James would be! Should Severo Cardenosa decide to go to England to square accounts with Bella . . .

Her mind refused to go on. Swiftly she turned ready to plead with him not to harm her sister, only to find to her utmost relief that she had no need to sink her pride, no need to beg him not to harm Bella.

'I don't recall saying I didn't find you a suitable substitute,' he drawled, his shuttered expression giving nothing away.

Reggie was careless what his thoughts were anyway, his words alone sent hope surging in her breast. 'You mean—you mean it will be all right? That you'll take me . . .'

'What do your parents think of your coming to Uruguay?' he interrupted, changing course so quickly she couldn't fathom what he was getting at.

'My parents?'

'Do they know exactly what you and your sister have been up to?'

Anger that he thought her parents wouldn't have cared less what she got up to, for that was what his tone implied, was again trying to take hold. She conquered it—just.

'My parents died when I was a child,' she said tonelessly. 'I was brought up by my grandparents.'

His eyes showed a flicker of interest. 'Your grandparents—they are living still?'

'No.' The woodenness of her expression softened as her thoughts dwelt briefly on those two kindly souls who without hesitation had taken her and Bella over. 'Grandfather died four years ago. My grandmother, though in the best of health when he died, loved him so dearly that neither Bella nor I were sufficient to make up for losing him, and she died six months later.'

She stopped there. Whether he had perceived how much she had loved them, she neither knew nor cared. But a short silence followed, then with another of those quick-changing moods she was getting to know he said suddenly, decisively:

'Right. You can pack after we've had lunch downstairs, then we'll get on our way.'

'You're taking me?' Oh, how she wished she hadn't asked! It was obvious from what he said, without the need of her impulsive question.

His right eyebrow ascended, a mocking look crossing his face. 'Yes, Reggie Barrington,' he answered. 'Oh yes, I'm taking you.'

Severo Cardenosa spoke very little on the short flight from the airport at Carrasco to Durazno, and Reggie was glad about that. Things had moved fast after his pronouncement that he was taking her. She had lost a load of her anxiety by the time they entered the restaurant for one thing, and as a consequence discovered she was hungry. But anxiety rushed in to take the pleasure with which she had been anticipating the gateau at the end of the meal, all pleasure disappearing as she suddenly realised she would have to say something about her hotel bill.

'Something the matter?'

She hadn't realised her face was as expressive as all that—or was it just that Severo Cardenosa was more observant than most? He was acid-sharp, she had found out that much, but . . .

'I—er—it occurred to me I shall—er—have to see Reception before we leave,' she got out, hoping she didn't look as hot and bothered as she felt. He wasn't helping one bit, she fumed silently, sure with the intelligence in the very look of him that he knew what she was getting at. 'I had to sell my car to afford my air fare,' she added tightly, ready to hit him right there in the dining room if he made just one single solitary crack about her being on the make—this being the first overture. 'It's left me with very little over,' she ended flatly, aware that her cheeks were scarlet at having to ask this man for money.

An age seemed to pass before he put her out of her misery. Casually he leaned back in his chair, his eyes going over her flushed cheeks, his survey thorough.

'Since it was I who made the booking, *mi querida*,' he said at last, 'naturally I shall attend to the bill.'

While she accepted that he would perhaps have to drop a few endearments her way when they were with his grandfather, it did nothing for her heightened colour to have him practising now with that seductive-sounding Spanish equivalent of the word 'darling'.

That mocking glint was in his eyes once more as he instructed, 'Relax, Reggie. From here on you are my responsibility.'

Not wanting to be his responsibility, not wanting the gateau either, that not many minutes earlier had looked

too delicious to resist, she promptly excused herself and
went to her room to pack.

That Severo could well afford the outlay he had so far
spent in the pursuance of making his grandfather happy
was further borne out when on leaving the plane at Durazno airport he led her to an expensive-looking Maserati.
The heat of the day was getting to her, that or since she
had some relief from her tensions, though she was fully
aware that there would be further tensions ahead when it
came to acting the loving fiancée to the full, she had to own
to feeling worn out, drained, as the car sped nearer to
Cerros de Cielo.

On the plane, belatedly, admitted, she had asked after
his grandfather's health—there had been too much else
going on for her to have had the chance before—but she
could have done without that tightly controlled look
coming about his mouth as he had asked nastily;

'Are you worried?'

She had determined then not to say another word until
she was spoken to. But since then her stubbornness had
been sawn at by the thought that if his grandfather had
not maintained the progress he had made in hospital,
then Severo's reply could well have been on account that
he himself was very worried about the old man.

The thought loosened her tongue and had her breaking
the car's constraining silence she felt oppressive even if he
didn't. 'Er—had I better know who else I shall be meeting—besides your grandfather, I mean?'

Briefly he turned, his glance flicking her, and she was
struck again by the brilliance of his blue eyes. Strangely,
for no reason, her heart pumped a hurried beat or two
before settling, making her ask before he could answer, if
indeed he intended to, and she could see no reason why
he shouldn't:

'Do you have parents—I mean a father, a . . .'

'I'll take the implication that you think I'm a bastard as read,' he told her sardonically, causing her to wonder if this engagement was going to be got through without her once boxing his ears. Then all ideas of thumping him went out of her head, because he was telling her, 'My parents drowned. Like you I was reared by grand-parents.'

After that a severe look about him told her he had decided to clam up, and it was beneath her dignity to enquire again about the members of his household. Though glancing at him, noting the way his thick black hair met the collar of the pale grey shirt he wore beneath his lightweight suit, she thought it incredible that she was engaged to the handsome brute.

Tiredness blurred her impressions as the Maserati tra-velled on, though she was aware the car had been climb-ing before it finally turned up a long drive. A house ap-peared as Severo slowed, a large white-painted establish-ment, tubs of flowers interspersed with sound-looking pillars which supported a sturdy-roofed open verandah.

Gathering her wits, she had time only to realise that this was where her actress of the year bit had to begin, then Severo was at her door.

'Welcome to the Estancia de Cardenosa,' he said, assisting her to her feet.

Then he was escorting her inside and her impressions were all hectic for a while. For with a babble of Spanish much too fast for her to comprehend, a woman of about fifty, drying her hands on her apron, followed by a much younger girl Reggie guessed to be about eighteen, was coming towards them.

Severo silenced the elder woman doing all the talking by a raise of his hand, though his white even teeth were in evidence as he told her—and here Reggie did under-stand, or thought she did—that he would apologise for putting her in such a flap with his telephone call another time, but meantime would she finish drying her hands and welcome his fiancée.

There wasn't time for her to check her translation, for Severo had turned to her, his right arm coming about her shoulders. '*Querida*, I would like you to meet Maria, who has looked after the house for as long as I can remember.'

Reggie extended her hand. '*Mucho gusto*, Maria,' she said, knowing her schoolgirl Spanish was showing.

'You speak Spanish?'

Severo's surprised question came at the end of Maria's voluble and only half understood reply, though since he had spoken in English, Reggie was hoping Maria hadn't understood and thought it an odd question for him to ask someone he knew well enough to be engaged to.

'A little,' she replied, and was then having the girl Juana introduced, and being told that Juana had been assigned to look after her.

Reggie repeated her Spanish 'How do you do' to the dark-haired girl whose shyly smiling brown eyes seemed to fill her face. Then Maria was informing Severo, as far as she could understand, that he had a visitor, that the Señora Gomez was here.

Who Señora Gomez was, Reggie didn't discover, though for a moment it looked as if Severo would take her with him to see the Señora. She felt his arm tighten on her shoulders as though to turn her in the direction of where Señora Gomez was waiting. Then he looked down into her face and must have judged, she thought, that she wasn't looking her best to meet his visitor, for his arm fell away and he was firing instructions at Juana, while Reggie was privately admitting that the scant sleep she had had since her arrival in Uruguay, not to mention the long flight from England, had finally caught up with her.

'Go with Juana,' Severo said, a gentle note there because they had an audience. 'It is our custom to dine late—perhaps a siesta would be welcome to you before then?'

Then before she knew what was happening, Juana was showing her to a room that had been prepared for her. And unbelievably, since she had never had such a service done for her before, she was accepting that Juana was helping her out of her clothes and a cool sheet was covering her.

Vaguely, sleep rapidly claiming her, she heard Juana tiptoeing from the room, and a smile of whimsy tugged her lips. Her last thought was that she had slotted into her new life style as to the manner born.

CHAPTER FOUR

REGGIE stirred, stretched, memory speeding in as she opened her eyes. London was six thousand miles away. She wasn't in bed in her flat, but here in Cerros de Cielo, the fiancée of one Señor Severo Cardenosa, a man she didn't think she cared very much for, yet a man she was going to have to pretend she thought wakened the sun each day.

Thoughts of Clive threatened at this juncture, probably because thoughts of being in love were synonymous with him. She mustn't think about Clive. Unless Irene divorced him she had no future with him, she knew that now—had known it when she had left London Airport. Though since he was due to arrive home that same day it hadn't stopped her from looking out for him, half hoping, she realised guiltily, that even at that late stage she might bump into him, that he might find out what she was doing and try to stop her going. Could she have denied him face to face?

She checked an anguished cry before it surfaced, forcing herself to eject Clive from her thoughts by contemplating her surroundings.

Her room was charming. Plain white walls relieved solid highly polished furniture, heavy lace curtains matched the lace of the bedcover, a couple of rose-coloured velvet-covered chairs in no way crowded the large airy room.

Reggie saw her suitcases had been brought in, but had no recollection of hearing a sound. Severo had said something about dinner being eaten late, so she had better get up and start with her loving fiancée act.

Opening one of her cases, she extracted a long cotton skirt and top together with fresh underwear. She assumed the other door in her room to be a bathroom, and her assumption proving correct, she showered and prepared to meet the man who was rapidly making her wish she had taken acting lessons. Trying to pretend she was in love with him was going to be no easy task.

She was ready when, silently as though not to disturb her if she was asleep, Juana appeared, to show her the way to the dining room. She took her along a wide hall that branched to the right into a wide corridor leading into the living area.

When at the door of the dining room, another large room with a long, long dining table, Reggie saw at once that only one place setting had been laid. Apparently she was to dine alone.

Well, she hadn't expected to see Grandfather Cardenosa at dinner; quite probably he had all his meals in his room. That meant she wouldn't meet him until tomorrow—which was strange, since she would have thought

Severo would want him to see her straight away. She had been tired, admittedly, Severo had seen that—though since she was not feeling very friendly towards him at that moment he earned no points from her for consideration. If it would have pleased Grandfather Cardenosa she wouldn't have minded one bit going along to see him.

Maria, bustling in with a tureen of soup accompanied by a burst of her fast flowing Spanish, broke into her musings. She thought Maria asked her if she had slept well as she ladled the delicious-smelling soup into her bowl.

'Yes, very well, thank you,' she answered in Spanish, and seeing Maria's beaming smile at her answer, congratulated herself that she had interpreted her question correctly.

Uruguayan servants, she discovered, knew no class distinction such as still existed in her own country. At least, Maria knew no such barrier, for as though seeing Reggie looked to be in need of company she stayed chatting while Reggie drank her soup, repeating words here and there that she didn't understand. It was in this way that Reggie got to know why she was dining alone. It seemed that after she had gone for her siesta, Severo had ridden over with Señora Gomez to the Gomez ranch.

Maria didn't appear to think it odd that he had stayed there or that Severo should leave his fiancée to her own devices on her first night in his home. But Reggie felt a distinct embarrassment, and was angered too. Here she was all set to carry out her part of Bella's bargain and with no fiancé to play Juliet to!

It further annoyed her when she found she was actually wondering just how old this Señora Gomez was. She wasn't interested, for goodness' sake—even if Señora Gomez didn't turn out to be old enough to be his mother. She certainly wasn't going to question Maria either, she determined. If he was having an affair—and since he obviously preferred to have his dinner at the Gomez table he could well be—then she wasn't going to have Maria thinking she was at all bothered by asking questions about the woman.

Instead she enquired after the health of Señor Cardenosa. and at Maria's puzzled expression realised she must have got her Spanish mixed up somewhere.

'The grandfather—how is he?' she tried again.

'Grandfather!' Maria exclaimed, and caused Reggie to be upset on Maria's behalf when tears appeared in her eyes. It was plain Maria was fond of Severo's grandfather, so naturally she would be upset that he would shortly be gone from them.

'You must mean Grandmother,' Maria confused her by saying, dabbing at her eyes with the corner of her apron. 'She is not good, but with the funeral only yesterday it is to be expected, I think.'

Reggie endeavoured to look sympathetc, knowing that between them the Spanish language had become hopelessly muddled. She had been patting herself on the back too that more and more of the tongue had been coming back to her. Somehow or other she must have mixed up her sexes, but to enquire into whose funeral—probably it had been a friend of the old man's—was just asking for more confusion.

Not thinking Maria would take it kindly if another mix-up of Spanish had her smiling while they were discussing a funeral, when the housekeeper went away to bring her her next course she decided a change of subject was called for when Maria showed every sign of staying while she ate her steak.

'My room is very lovely,' she said, cutting into the most mouthwatering steak she had ever tasted. 'Thank you, Maria, for getting it ready for me.'

Maria shrugged her thanks away, though she was smiling as she said, 'First you are coming and I am to prepare a room, then Doña Eva tells me fog in London has delayed you. Then Don Severo is telling me you are not coming at all, but I am not to tell Doña Eva.' Reggie's mind was boggling trying to translate this, much too busy then to query who Doña Eva was. 'Then today lunch time I am telephoned to say to drop everything and prepare the best room we have, for Don Severo is bringing with him his fiancée.'

Not at all sure she had translated everything correctly, Reggie was left to finish her meal alone when Juana appeared at the dining room door. Maria heard what Juana had to say—some minor crisis in the kitchen, Reggie gathered—then Maria was excusing herself to go with Juana. She was still going back over what had been said when Maria returned bearing a most mouthwatering-looking gateau.

'Don Severo said this is your favourite,' Maria said softly, her eyes warm at the love she thought her master and his fiancée shared, and causing Reggie to think he must have asked Maria to make the gateau specially for her.

It was a strawberry gateau like the one she had left at lunch when her appetite had disappeared so abruptly. More likely it was Severo's sardonic sense of humour showing through, she thought, than any desire he had that she shouldn't be done out of her strawberry gateau— he had known she hadn't cared to be claimed as his responsibility; was this one of his charming ways of endorsing that she was? She bit down the feeling of irritation with him, managing a smile for Maria as she thanked her for the trouble she had been to.

In bed that night, having been wide awake enough to tell Juana she could manage on her own, though thanking her for having unpacked her cases while she had been at dinner, Reggie allowed her mind to wander freely everywhere but on Clive.

She still couldn't get over Bella lying to her. She had never done so before, she was sure. Yet not telling Severo she was coming in her place had only served to underline how desperate she was. She must have been terrified he wouldn't agree to a substitute!

Really she should write and tell her everything was all right; she had sent a postcard from Montevideo ... Reggie was brought up short as she recalled how Bella had been going to tell James, having heard from her how lovely Uruguay was, that her younger sister, inheriting some money too—no doubt from the same ficticious relative who had left Bella ten thousand—had decided to spend some of it on seeing Uruguay for herself.

That Bella could lie so to James who was her whole world caused her to have more qualms about her sister's honesty, and her writing case stayed in the little writing desk where Juana had placed it. She would write to Bella tomorrow. Tonight, she just couldn't.

Her mind was a jumble of thoughts as drowsiness once more had her drifting towards sleep. Who was Doña Eva? She had never heard her mentioned before tonight. Was she another of Severo's girl-friends? He had a look about him that said he wasn't averse to playing the field when the mood was on him. She recalled almost his first words to her, 'Do I get a kiss of greeting?' He hadn't better start to try his hand with her, that was all—she had a trump card, didn't she? She would threaten to tell his grandfather everything if he thought to enter their 'engagement' as though it was for real.

Suddenly all thought of sleep left her at the remembrance of Maria telling her that up until lunch time today they hadn't been expecting her. Surely she must have got that wrong? But no, Severo had said just before he had introduced Maria that he would apologise later for putting her in such a flap with his phone call. He must have telephoned while she was packing to go with him.

She sat up, trying to get her thoughts in order. That could only mean that at the least he had been undecided about whether or not to bring her back. Though why come to see her in Montevideo at all? Of course, her telegram. He couldn't very well ignore her 'Can't wait to see you, darling', especially if his grandfather had seen her telegram, could he?

Reggie got down in the bed again, realising she could puzzle at it all night, but Severo was the only one who could give her any answers, and he must still be with the Gomez woman. She thumped her pillow, wishing it was his head. That she was here must mean that Grandfather Cardenosa still needed to have confirmation that an English fiancée existed. About the funeral Maria had spoken of she didn't bother her head; she had enough to keep her busy without delving into that.

She awoke, stretched and saw brilliant sunlight pouring into the room. Then any pleasure to be found on waking to such a morning fast evaporated as her eyes caught shadow where shadow should not have been.

'Good morning, my darling.'

Shaken rigid to hear that mocking voice in the privacy of her room, she was showing her amazement in the form of slightly parted lips when Severo Cardenosa stepped into her line of vision. Then to her astonishment, without another word being spoken, he leant over the bed, his head coming nearer and he sealed her mouth with his.

His hands on her shoulders, bare except for the flimsy straps of her nightdress, scorched her skin, and as her brain had not yet recovered it was instinctive to hold on to the check-sleeved arms on either side of her while the whirl in her brain sorted itself out.

Whether by that action Severo thought she was re-ciprocating, she didn't have time to ponder. But his hands moving to her back, his kiss becoming deeper, had her jerking away, pushing at him, her eyes dark blue and flaming with anger.

'How d-dare you! How dare you!' she spluttered, rage uppermost, her lips reserved for Clive.

Coolly, Severo straightened, her fury not affecting him in the slightest. 'I couldn't resist it,' he drawled. 'For ten minutes I've been waiting for you to wake. I have stood watching your loveliness, your beautiful blonde hair spread over your pillow, your lips even in sleep inviting, your . . .'

'Get out!' hotly she interrupted his flow. 'And don't ever come in here again!' It doubly annoyed her to find he had been watching her while she slept.

Her anger in no way cooled when instead of showing the least sign of his being in any way perturbed at being ordered out of any of the rooms in his own home, his blue eyes filled with unhidden amusement. It came as no sur-prise to hear him mock:

'Get out? Is that any way to talk to your *novio*?'

Fury threatened to take her reason that he was daring to laugh at her. Oh, if only she was fully dressed and not at the disadvantage of having to stay huddled in the bed-clothes!

'You may be my—*novio*—but it's only a temporary arrangement,' she raged, 'and that doesn't give you the right to think you can—can kiss me whenever you feel like it!'

'There's fire in you, my lovely—as I knew there would be,' he tormented, his eyes going appreciatively from her sparking blue eyes to where the bed sheet had slipped to reveal one deliciously satiny-skinned rounded shoulder.

Hastily Reggie drew the sheet up round her throat, almost choking herself in the process, incensed on catching the glint of laughter in his eyes at her attempt at modesty.

'Fire you will know nothing about,' she snapped, never having thought of herself as being fiery-blooded until he had aroused such anger. 'And,' she added, determined to sort this out here and now scantily clad as she was with him fully dressed—his working clothes, she guessed from his leather riding boots and cord trousers, 'and while we're on the subject I'll thank you to keep your kisses for those who want them!' Memory of him dining with the unknown Señora Gomez—on her first night in his home too—had the next words spurting from her: 'Otherwise I shall have no alternative but to—but to . . .' A hard look coming about him, all humour vanishing, had her faltering.

'Don't stop there.' His voice was cold, telling her he took threats from no one. 'Just what exactly will you do should another occasion arise when I find the invitation of your lips irresistible?'

If he thought she was going to back down then he had another think coming! She held the trump card, didn't she? Her face as sombre as his, still angry but with some of her heat gone, she looked straight into his unsmiling eyes.

'Should you at any time——' she hesitated; she couldn't very well say 'while your grandfather is alive'; that would hurt him, though why she should bother about his feelings was a mystery to her, 'during my stay, ever do such a—a thing again, then I shall feel fully justified in telling your grandfather everything.'

She had thought his face had looked hard before, but it looked positively ruthless as she finished issuing her ultimatum. His jaw tightened as if he was checking some strong emotion. She saw his hands clench momentarily as though he was getting a grip on his feelings. His eyes went past her and for a moment she had the feeling he had forgotten she was there. Then suddenly he had himself under control and was moving towards the bed. And just when she was beginning to have doubts about that self-control, her heart starting to flutter that no one would hear her screaming if he began to attack her, he sat down on the edge of the bed, giving her one stern look, noting her alarm and not above referring to it.

'My purpose in coming to your room was not with the intention of ravishing the delightful body that sheet does little to conceal,' he told her coldly. 'As for your threat,' he shrugged as though it was insignificant, 'you have doubtless forgotten an ace beats a king.'

Her eyes widened that he should so far read into her mind as to know she had been thinking in terms of trumping any move he made. 'An ace?' she choked, some premonition telling her she wasn't as bright as she thought she had been.

'Have you forgotten the bargain I made with your sister?' Her face whitened, her eyes wide and afraid suddenly. 'Make no mistake, little one, should you at any time attempt to thwart my plans, then Bella Usher *and* her husband will hear from me.'

'You can't—you wouldn't!' The words flew from her in panic, all the confirmation she needed there in his look.

'Enough of this threat and counter-threat,' he said disdainfully, as if now he had without too much effort chopped her down to size, the matter was now beneath him. He then dipped into the pocket of his shirt and passed to her the most exquisite diamond solitaire engagement ring. 'I purchased this yesterday while you were packing,' he informed her, causing her to remember that he had also telephoned Maria, so he had been quite busy while she had got her things together, but there was no time then to bring up the matter of the phone call and all the thoughts that had triggered off, because Severo was telling her to put it on.

'You want me to wear it when I meet your grandfather?' she questioned, knowing the answer but needing time to get over the peculiar feeling of shyness that came over her, preventing her from putting on this wildly expensive item while he was there.

'You will wear it all the time,' he commanded, and, impatient with her dithering taking the ring from her, he pushed it on her engagement finger.

She was unused to wearing a ring on that finger, but the odd sensation it gave was blunted by the look of satisfaction on his face.

'Now,' he said, his face thoughtful, 'we come to the purpose of my visit.'

'It wasn't to—to give me this?' she enquired, holding up her left hand. He had already said it wasn't with the purpose of ravishing her either, she recalled, and she was at a loss to know what other reason he had. Her eyes showed her question as she looked at him.

'I must apologise for not coming to Montevideo to get you sooner,' he began. 'Penniless as you were, you must have had an anxious time.'

Colour flooded her cheeks at his turn of phrase, for all it was next door to the truth. 'There was some good cause why you couldn't come before?' she queried, instinct sharp in her suddenly, telling her there was a very good cause.

But when, not allowing an atom of emotion to show itself, Severo told her of that reason, she very nearly collapsed with the shock of it.

'A very good cause,' he confirmed. 'The day on which you arrived in Uruguay was the day on which my grandfather died.'

For several seconds she just looked at him with nothing happening in her brain at all, then, 'Died?' she whispered, then as remembrance of how much she had loved her own grandparents, how sad she had been when they had died, how much he must have loved his own grandfather, 'Oh, Severo,' she said softly, 'I'm so sorry.' Then as her brain roared into life, working apart from the emotion of that sad moment, bewilderment took the sharpness off her words. 'But—but if your grandfather is dead, then—then what on earth am I doing here?'

For long moments he looked back without speaking. He knew already from her initial reaction to his news that he had her sympathy, but his face was still expressionless as he at last said:

'As you can imagine, my grandmother is very distraught.'

'*Grandmother?*' Her startled exclamation said it all. She had assumed his grandmother to be dead—and yet . . . She recalled the mixed-up conversation she had had with Maria last night, and as everything fell into place she realised it wasn't so very mixed up after all. 'I didn't realise your grandmother was still alive,' she tacked on quietly. 'Maria mentioned a Doña Eva—is she your grandmother?'

He nodded. 'Like you, she is English.' He paused briefly before going on, 'You, Reggie, will be a great source of comfort to her. As I said, she is distraught. She and Grandfather had been together for sixty years.' Reggie's heart went out to her. 'But,' he paused again as though it pained him to have to talk on the subject but was having to do so because there were things she had to know, 'but in her distress there is something that keeps her from giving in.'

A heavy weight she didn't want to have to carry was descending on Reggie, and she just knew she wasn't going to like the answer before she asked:

'And that something is?'

'The comfort she is gaining from the knowledge that her beloved Roberto died happy.'

'Because of this—our engagement?'

'They were everything to each other,' he said bleakly. 'What she wanted, he wanted for her. What he wanted, she wanted too.' He stood up as though needing action to control his own unhappiness in losing the man who had brought him up, and went to stare out of the window.

There was silence in the room which she just couldn't intrude upon by breaking into the sadness of his thoughts. But that didn't stop her mind from ticking over. It should simply be a case of no grandfather, no engagement, she thought. But she was certain Severo hadn't brought her here just for the purpose of telling her his grandfather had passed away. He could have done that in Montevideo! Why, not many minutes ago he had given her this beautiful engagement ring. She looked down at her hand, seeing yet not seeing the solitaire, every sense telling her exactly why she was wearing his ring. And then she just had to break into his private grief, had to voice the certainty that was growing within her.

'You still want me to pretend to be engaged to you don't you? This time for your grandmother's sake.'

His expression when he turned had changed very little. 'At the moment the *only* solace Abuela has in her grief is that because my *novia* would soon be here, her dear one departed with joy in his heart.'

Reggie knew then she just couldn't add to the old lady's mental suffering, though she wished almost desperately that she had a harder heart. She kicked against the knowledge that had it been her own grandmother she, like Severo, would have done anything rather than cause her a moment's pain.

But she mustn't allow sentiment, her soft heart, to cloud the vision of her thinking. Her stay in Uruguay had been said to be not very long because of Grandfather Cardenosa's weakened state of health. Doña Eva might be a robust lady, the sort who had never had a day's illness in her life.

Unconsciously she sighed. Her personal wish to get back to England with all speed was at odds with this, constant it seemed to her, desire to know how soon all Severo's elderly relatives were likely to pop off.

'Er—how long is this—er—new arrangement likely to be for?' she asked, hating the embarrassment of having to ask such a question, especially at a time like this.

'My grandmother is eighty. You will see for yourself how frail she looks,' he said, not by a flicker of an eyelash showing any emotion that she had all but agreed. 'The love my grandparents had for each other was, I think, of the same quality your own grandparents shared.'

'And my grandmother couldn't endure to live without Grandfather,' Reggie put in, her eyes moist, remembering as she said the words she had already told him, 'she died six months after him.'

She blinked to clear the signs of emotion from her eyes, knowing there was very little more to be said. It was less than useless calling herself all kinds of a fool. It wasn't in her to upset the old lady at such a time—to add to her grief by disengaging herself from Severo. It just wasn't in her.

'When am I to meet her?' she asked, carefully keeping all sign of emotion out of her voice.

But if she lacked any sign of emotion, then for the first time in an age emotion came to Severo's face. It took the shape of a half smile that caused her to hope those weren't traces of triumph she saw there.

'As you can see,' he said, referring to the way he was dressed, 'I have one or two matters to attend to. I have told Ana, Abuela's maid, that we will visit at eleven. You will be ready?'

'Your grandmother lives here?' Reggie wasn't quite sure why she asked, because she hadn't questioned that his grandfather lived with him.

'For the moment. If she recovers her strength then it is possible she will want to return to her own home, not far away—we shall have to wait and see.'

Reggie spent the time in waiting for Severo to take her to meet his grandmother in showering, dressing in one of her better dresses, a coffee-coloured linen, having a solitary breakfast and wondering what she had got herself into now. One thing was for sure, with the old lady being English, she had better watch out that she didn't make a slip anywhere. She wouldn't be able to put any impulsive verbal attack on Severo—who had the greatest knack of rattling her to sudden fury quicker than anyone she had ever met—down to a faulty translation. English was Doña Eva's native tongue too.

She had time while she was waiting to realise that Maria's, 'Don Severo telling me you are not coming at all,' must in part at least be put down to an error in translation. He had already told Doña Eva that fog had delayed her, and she could see the reason for him doing so in the circumstances. What with the household being upset with the death of his grandfather, it would be easier to let her think she had been delayed by fog than have her arrive on a day that must have been a great strain for the old lady.

The last minutes before Severo came for her seemed to drag by at a snail's pace. Purposely, needing time to compose herself, she had avoided leaving the house, but as she gazed from her bedroom window out at green, green lawns and borders where every conceivable flower appeared to be growing, she knew she would far rather be out there in the peace and tranquillity of the scene than about to face what she was about to face.

A sound of her door being opened behind her alerted her to the fact Severo had come for her. She turned, knowing she mustn't allow herself to get annoyed that he seemed to not have heard of such a small courtesy as knocking on a door before entering. She needed all her composure for the coming interview.

As coolly as she could she looked at him, noting again his height, the insolent way he wore his good looks. She observed that he had changed into a lightweight pale grey suit, and sought with her eyes for her handbag. No need to take it with her, of course, she wasn't leaving the house, but she felt the need for something to hang on to.

Severo didn't say whether he thought she looked presentable in her coffee-coloured linen, for all she saw his eyes had missed nothing in his inspection. In fact he had very little to say at all except one word.

'*Venga.*' It was the Spanish for 'Come'.

CHAPTER FIVE

SHE saw at once from where Severo had inherited his brilliantly blue eyes. The sitting room of the suite of rooms Doña Eva occupied was cool and shaded, but even with the light less powerful here she saw that not only had the years barely faded those blue eyes, but that those eyes were moist as Severo made the introduction.

Another thing she couldn't help noticing was how

very gentle Severo was with the elderly lady. 'Abuela,' his voice soft and caring, 'let me introduce your future granddaughter.'

There was little time then for her to mentally object to being introduced this way—it sounded more final than if he had said 'Let me introduce you to my fiancée' for even as he was following up with, 'Reggie, *querida*—my grandmother,' the little old lady, against her murmur of protest, was rising from her chair.

It was instinctive then, as two thin arms came out towards her, for Reggie to go forward. Instinctive too, since the old lady did look as frail as Severo had said, for her to hold her as Doña Eva embraced her, her once smooth cheek, now aged, pressed up against her own.

'You've chosen well, Severo.' Doña Eva at length pulled back, the tears Reggie witnessed in her eyes bringing a choking sensation to her throat as the faultless English accent met her ears. 'Abuelo would have been so proud of your choice,' she sighed. Emotion was thick in the air while Reggie sought for something to say. And then Doña Eva had recalled, 'But you did meet Severo's grandfather, did you not, Regina?'

Remembering Bella had gone to see the old man in hospital, Reggie could have wished Severo would step in and help her out, because she was finding it totally impossible to lie to the old lady.

'I was so sorry when Severo told me your husband had died,' she said gently, and found her hands warmly squeezed.

Severo saw his grandmother back into her chair, suggesting, with a loving look at his fiancée that she knew meant nothing, 'Perhaps you would like to sit here by Abuela.'

Doing her best to emulate his loving look as she took the chair next to Doña Eva, Reggie saw he looked slightly surprised to find she was entering into the spirit of the pretence, and her eyes quickly found something to admire in the cream-coloured carpet. Well, what did he expect, for goodness' sake, she mused crossly, that she should further upset his grandmother by telling him to go to hell? Already she was hating this deception, yet with Doña Eva looking so fragile, her loss so new, she wouldn't have dreamt of adding to her distress.

Doña Eva's maid Ana came quietly into the room, and talk while the maid served them with coffee was of Reggie's flight, Doña Eva saying that though she loved London and had visited the capital many times over the years, a London fog was something she tried to avoid.

As silently as she had entered the room, Ana withdrew, and a few minutes were passed in quiet conversation, none of them shying from mentioning Doña Eva's husband since she appeared to have a need to feel he was still with them, still a part of them.

As she had found everything going smoother than she had dared to hope, Reggie's nerves and apprehensions faded as conversation became easier. Then suddenly Doña Eva visibly brightened.

'And now,' she said, her smiling glance taking in Reggie and Severo both seated near, 'we have to look forward to happier times.'

Not knowing what was coming, Reggie tried to keep her face composed, a be-ready-for-anything instruction being sent up to her brain. But her brain just wasn't ready to receive what followed, and all her nerves and apprehensions jangled together in one agitated mass, when Doña Eva said:

'Roberto and I had many years together, many years in which to store up such happy memories. Now it's the turn of you and Severo to begin to make your memories.' Her glance stayed on Reggie, her eyes tender. 'I was more delighted than I can say when Severo told me earlier this morning that last night you arranged your wedding date for the twenty-fourth of this month.'

'*Twenty-fourth!*'

Severo was in there before she could tell his grand-mother what a lying hound he was. Last night he had been with the Gomez woman. He was out of his chair, an arm coming around her shoulders in a hard warning grip that hurt.

'Still exhausted from your flight, *querida*?' he teased, only his flint-hard eyes showing the insincerity of his teas-ing. 'You were awake enough last night when you told me the next three weeks can't go fast enough for you.'

'I—er——' Reggie floundered, knowing she would have to pull herself together.

She glanced at Doña Eva, saw her pale face, a fresh wrinkle on her brow as though they were confusing her, and felt so dreadfully sorry for her. Her husband hadn't been dead a week yet. She just had to go along with it, even if it did mean lying her head off. Anything to get the old lady smiling again and looking less as though she might suffer a heart attack at the smallest shock.

'I—er—didn't know you were going to tell your grandmother so soon, darling,' she murmured. 'I'm sorry —er——' she hesitated, not quite sure what to call the old lady and settled for, 'Doña Eva. Of course, as Severo says, I——' and in up to her neck, 'I'm looking forward to my —our wedding day. It's just that I thought you might be offended as it's so near to . . .'

By this time Doña Eva was smiling again in full sym-pathy with her future granddaughter-in-law's sensitivities. 'Oh, my dear,' she said gently, 'I'm not at all offended that you and Severo want to be married so soon after Roberto's death. And it would please me if you would call me Abuela as Severo does.' She sent Severo a loving look that was full of pride for the tall good-looking man she had helped to rear, then went on, 'Severo made his grandfather the happiest of men when he told him he was to marry an English girl. Because of Severo's news Roberto was able to die knowing his last wish was to come true. Believe me, he would applaud Severo's decision to waste no time in making you his wife.'

Feeling trapped, all Reggie could do was to smile and hope her smile wasn't as sickly as she felt. Then the man who for his own reasons was threatening to make her his bride before the next three weeks were out, if she didn't do something about it, rose to his feet.

'I think you have had enough excitement for one morning, Abuela,' he said gently, going over to kiss the old lady's wrinkled cheek. 'Reggie and I will come and see you again—for the moment we will leave you.'

She was left alone with Doña Eva while Severo went in search of Ana. But she had no need to search for anything to say, spontaneity having left her a few minutes ago, for Doña Eva was saying:

'I usually rest in the afternoon for an hour or so, but if you are free around four perhaps you would join me for tea?'

Smiling, Reggie accepted the invitation, powerless to do anything else and realising it was natural for her to want them to know each other better.

'I'll look forward to it,' she said, wishing the circumstances were different and that she had no need to feel anxious about the four o'clock meeting.

'May I call you Reggie too?' Doña Eva was asking.

'I'd like that,' Reggie was replying—her first honest answer in a long while, she was thinking. Then Severo was back, his arm once more around her shoulders.

'Ready, *querida*?'

Knowing the urge to knock that smile off his face

would have to wait, she picked up her bag and made her farewells to Doña Eva.

But once out in the hall and away from where they could be overheard, she angrily shrugged out of the arm which had remained about her shoulders.

'Don't touch me!' she snapped, dynamite in her anger needing only the merest spark to have it exploding. 'Don't you ever, *ever* touch me again!'

'That might prove a little difficult,' came the laconic answer, which did nothing to lengthen the fuse on her fury that he could sound so complacent when she was ready to give forth with an eruption that would put Vesuvius to shame.

The explosion nearly happened out there in the hall, for after walking to where the hall angled, though stomping would have been a more apt description of the way Reggie set her feet, seeing she could find her own way to her room, as cool as you like to her mind, Severo said:

'If you'll excuse me, I have work that calls for my attention in my study.'

And while she stood rooted, dumbfounded that he thought he could just announce their wedding date and that was all there was to it, he gave a slight bow in her direction and strode away.

'*Just one minute!*' Her voice, that she had never known possessed such a roar, bellowed after him.

He halted, turned, and if just one single solitary smile had cracked his face, then Reggie knew at that moment that regardless of the consequenses, she would have flown at him, for she was sure there was a look of devilment in his eyes.

'I have one or two things I should like to say to you,' she told him, her voice only marginally quieter.

For a second or two he surveyed her mutinous face, her eyes flashing fire. 'Might I suggest,' he said eventually, 'that if you intend to scream like a . . .' he paused to get the correct English expression, 'fishwife, then perhaps you should join me in the privacy of my study.'

That he should take it she would follow him as he casually turned back to the way he had been going and walk on to open his study door and go through had her anger boiling over. She was in that same room, hardly aware she had charged after him, not bothering to close the door after her.

Unperturbed, Severo went unhurriedly to shut it, but even while he was closing it, she was laying into him.

'What do you mean by telling your grandmother I'd agreed to marry you?' she stormed. 'You know damn well I never so much as clapped eyes on you last night!' Her cheeks were hot with her fury, she didn't like it one bit that he just propped himself up on his desk, folded his arms in front of him, and made no attempt to defend himself. He seemed set if anything to lean there until she had burnt herself out. 'What the hell do you mean by it?' she demanded to know. 'You're as aware as I am that you couldn't wait to pack me off to my room so you could continue your—your liaison with that Gomez woman!'

'Liaison? Gomez woman?' Severo echoed, his eyes suddenly alert before, infuriatingly, a smile did cross his face as he accused, 'Reggie, you're jealous!' His smile became a laugh as his head tipped back and a deep-throated shout of laughter left him. 'Without ever having seen—the Gomez woman, you are jealous of her.'

'I am not jealous!' she raged, only just this side of aiming a kick at his shin to see how funny he thought that was. 'Don't be ridiculous,' she snapped. 'I just—just happen to think it very bad form to dump me in your home as though I'm some unwanted p-parcel, that's all.'

Severo sobered at being accused of being ill-mannered, his pride evident as his arms unfolded and he stood away from his desk. 'I apologise,' he said stiffly. 'If you have been made to feel like a—parcel—that was not my intention at all. My visit to the Gomez home was necessary, otherwise I certainly should not have left you. Though in all fairness I think you will agree you were near to the point of exhaustion and, I think, feeling you had had sufficient of my company for one day.'

He was turning the tables on her and she didn't like it. 'Well,' she said, lamely realising some of her heat had left but determined not to be on the defensive, 'that doesn't alter the fact that you've added to the lies you've told your grandmother. I have no intention of marrying you and you know it.'

Levelly he looked at her. Then instead of telling her why he had told his grandmother this latest lie, he further shattered her by denying it was a lie at all.

'I may have stretched the truth here and there,' he told her coolly, 'all in the attempt to give her a little peace of mind in this very difficult period of her mourning. But I certainly wasn't lying when I told her that I would be marrying Regina Barrington on the twenty-fourth of this month.'

Shaken rigid, for there was a conviction about him that said he meant every word, Reggie opened her mouth, found her throat had dried up, and her eyes wide with incredulity, she tried again.

'But—but I never said I'd marry you!' she denied.

Severo flattened her composure before it could get a firm hold. 'A girl calling herself Regina Barrington did.'

'You mean Bella agreed to marry you?' she gasped, her disbelief evident.

'It would appear your sister misled you in more than one detail. She told you she had advised me that you were coming in her place, when she had not,' he reminded her.

Feeling winded, Reggie could only look at him, wide-eyed, struck dumb as the truth of what he was saying hit her. Then remembering the love Bella had for James, she didn't know what to believe. Surely loving James as she did Bella wouldn't agree to marry another man? Yes, but, prompted a small voice, there was a vast difference between agreeing to marry someone and actually going through with it. Bella hadn't hesitated to break her contract to be Severo's fiancée when her love for James had got on top of her. All the same, her lovely sister wouldn't . . .

'Bella wouldn't . . .' she began to defend, only to have her words chopped in mid-air as though he was tired of the whole argument.

'There's the telephone,' he said, pointing to the instrument. 'Put through a call and ask her.'

Her hand went to the phone before she realised the futility of trying to get through. 'Bella's on her honeymoon,' she said, and, her intelligence at work, 'as you well know. You know too that even if I could contact her I wouldn't, because you still hold that ace, don't you?'

He didn't deign to answer. 'I paid ten thousand pounds for a bride,' he said instead. 'I have every intention of having a bride, Regina Barrington.'

'I'm not going to marry you.' Her temper was coming again, helping her out of the feeling she was fighting a losing battle. 'So don't you think for a moment that I am!'

His face hardened, but not so much, she thought, because it wasn't every day or any day he got turned down. She soon found out the cause for the hard look he was giving her.

'What are you after?' he asked unpleasantly. 'More money?'

'More money?'

'Trying to up the price. Perhaps you too are after ten thousand to put into your bank account.'

Vesuvius erupted. Her stinging hand, the cruel grip of his hands on her arms as he shook her, told her she had hit him and that he was furious about it.

'No, I'm not!' she was shouting, terrified by the demoniacal look on his face that soon she would have a similar red mark to match the one he had showing on her cheek. Her good sense left her then in her fear of him, and she was babbling more than she would have let anyone know other than Bella. 'I'm not interested in your money. I c-can't marry you, Severo—how can I? I'm in love with another man!'

The grip on her arms threatened to crush her bones as her confession rang through the air. He was livid, she could see that, but she knew it wasn't because she had confessed her love for another man, but because he had decided he would marry her and was furious at her repeated refusal. Fear beset her again as his eyes burned into her, his mouth taking a cruel line, his eyes harder than she had ever seen them, like chips of flaming granite.

It was only as a cry of pain came from her that he seemed to realise how violently he was treating her. His hands dropped to his sides, but his face was still hostile.

'We will discuss this matter again,' he told her shortly. 'Deny our forthcoming wedding to my grandmother when you see her this afternoon and both you and your precious sister will live to regret it.'

It barely registered that his grandmother must have told him she was inviting her to take tea with her that afternoon, because he hadn't been there when the invitation had been issued, for she was too busy trying to keep herself from wilting. Wanting badly to answer back, she found any words she had were stuck fast in her throat.

He obviously wasn't expecting her to say anything, taking her silence for acquiescence anyway. And what he had to do in his study could not have been as important as it had once seemed, for without saying another word he strode to the door as if he didn't trust himself, his anger, with her in the same room, and left her alone with her own mixed-up thoughts.

Damn him, damn him! Damn him to hell, Reggie fumed, her fury returning when it didn't look as though he was coming back to set about her. It was some minutes before she too left the study—minutes which had been filled completely with railing against him.

If anything, prior to knowing Severo Cardenosa, she would have said her nature was on the placid side. But since knowing him it was fast being brought home that the fire he had said she possessed was a fact. Oh, not the sexual fire she was sure was behind his remark, but fire of such flaming anger she had for the first time in her life physically set about someone.

Not that he hadn't had it coming. No man had so moved her to such fury before. If she had had time to think before she had acted, she would have hit him harder. It was all his fault, unquestionably all his fault, she fumed, her feet of their own volition taking her out on to the verandah.

And it was on the verandah that fair play prodded for a hearing, the thought that Bella wasn't coming out of this smelling exactly of violets disquieting her. Bella had lied once before. She had believed her when she said Severo had agreed to her coming in her stead, when he had known nothing about it. Just as she had believed her when she had said all she had to do was pretend to be his fiancée for a few months. Had Bella lied again?

Remembering that her sister had looked desperate enough to do anything, Reggie felt the need to clear her muddled head, to be away from the house. Collecting her sunglasses from her room, she returned to the verandah, wondering which way to go.

The Estancia de Cardenosa stood on top of a hill, and glancing about she saw some outbuildings some way away from the house. That way was out. She had a feeling Severo Cardenosa might be over by those buildings, and she had no wish to see him again until it could possibly be avoided.

She took the opposite direction, passing a swimming pool, ignoring its cooling-looking waters in the noonday heat, passing lawns and flower beds. The worry of her present predicament had not let up, but as her feet took her through a field of lush grasses, some of the heat of her anger against her temporary fiancé, soon to be her husband—over her dead body!—had cooled.

She recalled how Bella had been after she had told her of the practical joke phone call. Some practical joke! How could she ring her and question her about this latest development? If Bella became as demented by her phone call as she had been then, James was bound to know something was wrong, might even get it out of her, and that would be the end of the marriage.

Her mind deeply involved, she faced the impossibility of ringing Bella; she had plenty of time before the twenty-fourth. But contacting Bella wasn't on, that didn't need too much thinking about; she couldn't bear to have her sister's ruined marriage on her conscience.

Lifting her head as though seeking inspiration, she saw a line of trees in the distance, and the shade they would afford drew her towards them, her mind too full to care what else lay around her.

But it was as she reached the belt of trees that contemplation of her present problems ceased, there being no room in her head for anything but to stand enraptured by the most beautiful scene she had ever set eyes upon. Even the least ardent nature-lover would have been captivated, and she was far from being one of those.

A warm wind fanned her face, stirred the pale green arms of a weeping willow, had the leaves of a sycamore whispering to each other, and played a rippling tune on a stream that tinkled, glinting in sunlight a yard from her feet.

This was no place where worries could be chewed over. The very beauty of it shook its head in reproach that anything should come to spoil it. With room only in her heart for delight, Reggie took off her sunglasses, since their lenses did not give her a true picture of the glorious colour all about. The soil around, so rich in potash, appeared almost black in colour, and her eyes swept on across the clear crystal waters of the stream to the other side, seeing where meadows of grassland flourished, giving off a bluish tinge, holding her breath as a hare raced through an abundance of wild flowers. The name Uruguay meant purple land, but aside from the purple flowers that coloured the landscape, she was able to pick out wild marigold, even a pink lupin that must have set itself on the wind.

It was picturesque, filled her senses, and she couldn't look enough. Yet she did, because each blink of an eye revealed something she had missed. Close by was a magnificent wild rose, happy to have dainty daisies rioting at its feet, a perfume greeting her nose, innocent yet exotic, a smell reserved for only old-fashioned roses.

Cerros de Cielo was aptly named, the thought came as she turned to look back at the house. It stood on the highest hill around. Bella had told her that nowhere in Uruguay did the land rise above two thousand feet—it didn't need to; mountains weren't necessary, everything was captured in its untamed rising and falling beauty.

This was the interior, and to Reggie's mind at that moment, it was magical.

But as she turned to look back at the house, some of the magic vanished. She had no idea how long she had been standing there entranced, or indeed at what point her worries about Bella, James, and most of all this latest turn of events in her temporary relationship with Severo, had gone from her mind, but she would have to find an answer to her problems somewhere.

She had better get back. Somehow, she didn't particularly care how he did it, but Severo was going to have to tell his grandmother that there had been a change in their wedding plans. He would be gentle with the old lady, she had no qualms on that score. He had treated her this morning as though she were a delicate piece of Dresden china.

Suddenly Reggie knew she couldn't go through with her visit to Doña Eva that afternoon, not unless Severo had told his grandmother first. With this in mind she didn't linger over her farewell to the beautiful place she had found, but hastened back up the hill, hoping against hope that Severo had returned to his study.

Sweat was sticking her dress to her back when she hurried into the hall, the thick walls of the *estancia* a cooling contrast to the heat outside. Before she had taken more than a few steps, however, Juana appeared, the relief on her face when she saw her making it plain she had been looking for her.

'Doña Regina . . .' she began, only for her voice to fade as Severo came round a bend in the hall, dismissing her quietly, his gaze never leaving his hot and bothered looking fiancée, damp tendrils starting to curl on her forehead.

'We have been looking for you, *querida*,' he said, coming to take her arm, the *querida* she knew because Juana was still within earshot.

'Severo, I wanted to have a word . . .' Reggie began, her earlier animosity with him forgotten in the urgency of what she had to say.

'Your word can wait. First, I think, a long cool drink is what you need.'

Not allowing her to utter another word, he escorted her to the *sala*, a cool room that housed several couches and easy chairs, telling her she must allow herself to become acclimatised to the heat of the day before she went rushing around.

Again, as he saw her seated, the spate of words which would have spilled out had to be held back. For Juana arrived with a much-needed glass of iced orange, making Reggie realise Severo must have requested it when dismissing Juana, only she had been too full of what she wanted to say to bother with the translation.

As Juana departed, as much because it was expected of her as her need, Reggie took a satisfying gulp from the glass in her hand.

'Perhaps until you have your bearings it will be as well if you tell someone in which direction you are going when you leave the *estancia*,' he suggested, a small reprimand, she thought, not feeling very comfortable to have him still standing while she was sitting.

'I'm sorry, I didn't think,' she apologised stiffly. It seemed to her as though he was saying she had to ask his permission to go out, a thorn in the side of her spirit of independence.

'No harm done.' He gave her a smile in which she might have found a deal of charm had she not got round to thinking that that smile, and the charm with it, was going to disappear when she asked him what she had every intention of asking. 'I doubt you would have got yourself lost, not so that we couldn't have found you anyway.'

If he was trying to make up for his earlier bad temper by being so pleasant, it was wasted on Reggie, who had seen that blazingly furious side to him. She took another, less thirsty, sip of orange and placed her glass on a nearby table.

'Severo . . .'

'Where did you go?' he asked, ignoring that she had an urgent need to ask him something.

The scene she had just left came back to her. 'Down to the stream,' she told him, and the colourful vista she had seen down there was just too much for her, the urgency of her question fading. 'Oh, Severo, it was so beautiful there! I could have wept from the pure magic of it.'

At once a feeling of having revealed too much of herself in her emotional words took her. Her eyes fell to her lap, a tinge of pink creeping over her cheeks. Unaware that Severo had moved, she felt his hand beneath her chin tipping her head where he could see into her eyes.

'The beauty of the place you found, *querida*,' he said softly, with no one there but her to hear the endearment, 'would be even more magical to have your beauty in its midst.'

And while she could only sit and stare, for his compliment to her had the sincerest ring, he bent and placed a gentle kiss on her upturned mouth.

It was a light fleeting kiss, a kiss she would afterwards wonder had it really happened. For it seemed more as though he was saluting her beauty than allowing anything sexual to disturb the moment. Then he straightened.

'When you have rested sufficiently, Maria is waiting to serve your lunch. I am afraid I have to go out, but tonight, Reggie, you and I will share dinner together.'

He had gone, and her fingers were straying as though mesmerised to her lips before the annoying thought came—he had gone! And just as though he knew she had a vital request to put to him, gone without giving her a chance to voice it!

CHAPTER SIX

Her feeling of resentment that Severo must have had a very good idea what she had wanted to ask, and had deliberately refused to allow her to put her request, had dimmed as the hour drew near when she was to go to tea with his grandmother. Uppermost then was the giant fear of saying the wrong thing.

She was such a hopeless liar. She hadn't any idea of the sort of questions Doña Eva might ask, so she couldn't even rehearse one or two white lies that then might have the ring of authenticity when she trotted them out. And what was she to do if she experienced another moment like that one this morning when she had found it absolutely impossible to lie to the sweet old lady?

Four o'clock came and with trepidation in her heart she left her room. The maid Ana answered her knock and must, Reggie guessed, have been with her employer for some years, for she said politely in English, making her feel more of a criminal than ever that she had given serious thought to pleading a headache and not coming at all:

'Doña Eva had so been looking forward to your visit.'

'My dear!' Seeing the old lady about to rise, Reggie hurried forward to prevent her, bending to kiss the proffered pale cheek. 'Ana has left the chair where she placed it this morning, so you can sit near.' Doña Eva settled back and when her guest was seated, continued, 'She'll bring tea presently, which I have sent from London. I expect you've tasted the *maté* which most Uruguayans drink, but I'm sure you won't mind a cup of "English" tea.'

Agreeing, Reggie couldn't help but be struck by the brightness of her hostess, though she hoped she wouldn't pay by being debilitated later if it was a determined effort to put her grief behind her on her behalf.

For a while Severo was barely mentioned, probably because Reggie thought it unwise to get bogged down in this area, and she told Doña Eva about her walk and all she had seen that morning.

'I can see already that you are learning to love this country as I love it,' Doña Eva said softly, going on, seeing Reggie's interest to tell her that Uruguay was made up of nineteen counties, called departments, Durazno being one of them.

'And I should imagine the prettiest,' put in Reggie, who couldn't imagine anywhere to be more enthralling than her place down by the stream.

'I think so, but then I'm biased,' Doña Eva smiled, and went on to tell her that Uruguay was founded on the eastern bank of the Rio de la Plata, the river Plate, and had because of this, until it became an independent state in 1828, been called La Banda Oriental, but the loveliest river to see, in her view, was the river Yi that bounded part of the department of Durazno. Her eyes clouded over at mention of the river Yi, causing Reggie to wonder if it was in that river that Severo's parents had drowned. She discovered it was, as Doña Eva told her how her son and daughter-in-law had perished in a freak accident while out sailing.

Anxious in case Doña Eva should become too distressed, Reggie suddenly realised that memories, even sad ones, were most of what the old lady had now. So instead of trying to divert the conversation, she listened, as she had many times to her own grandmother, and heard of things that had happened many years before.

'Severo was no more than a boy when he lost his parents,' she reminisced. 'Roberto and I have our own home, as you probably know. Naturally we took Severo to stay with us. But he was never happy away from his valleys and hills. So since Roberto loved this place too, we moved here for some years. Severo later went to university and when he returned he was a man. Roberto said then that we had done all we could, it was time now for Severo to be on his own.'

'Didn't Severo mind your going?' Reggie asked, thinking how he must have missed them, and then as Doña Eva's eyes sparkled brightly, she saw something of the beautiful girl she must have been.

'Not a bit of it,' she said wickedly. 'As Roberto had said, Severo was a man. I rather think he would have found it a mite irksome to have his old grandparents breathing down his neck every time he came home after a night's mischief!'

Reggie had to chuckle too, and felt a tenderness for this lady who had taken the changing times in her stride. But Doña Eva's expression was serious when she said, 'But word would get back to us of who was our grandson's latest and longest lasting lady-friend. As the years passed Roberto and I would think "Is this the one?" but no, never did he come to us and tell us he intended to marry. His grandfather so wanted him to be married, to have the fulfilled family life we had, and his parents had for a short time. Last year, on Severo's thirty-sixth birthday, Roberto gave him a stern lecture, telling him it was about time he settled down to a family life.'

The conversation taking this turn had nerves starting

to flutter inside Reggie. She just knew that at any time now the subject of her engagement was going to come up, and she just didn't have any idea how she was going to handle it. Desperately she tried to find a subject that would change the conversation, but anxious as she was to avoid upsetting Doña Eva, nothing else would penetrate but that she mustn't put a foot wrong.

'Your husband's lecture must have spurred Severo on,' she said, fiercely reminding herself that it was an engagement, a temporary engagement, that was all.

'I doubt it,' smiled Doña Eva. 'Severo told him then that he would marry only when he fell in love.'

Good, she thought. If he keeps his word to his grandfather, then I shan't have any problems. She felt better suddenly, for surely Severo must never have intended marriage between them to happen—he had just told Doña Eva that to brighten her spirits this morning, she felt sure. There were almost three weeks to go before the supposed wedding, and by that time Doña Eva would be well enough to be told there was a hitch or whatever story Severo chose to dream up.

'You will wear white, won't you?' Doña Eva asked suddenly.

'White?' As Reggie had just settled in her mind that there wasn't going to be a marriage, the question caught her on the hop.

'For your wedding, my dear. So many young people think it smart not to these days, don't they?'

'Er—yes,' she answered, and wasn't quite sure what she had answered yes to. Had she merely agreed that some girls preferred not to marry in white, or, from the smiling look on Doña Eva's face, had she entered deeper into deceiving her, so far as to saying her dress on the day she married Severo would be a white one?

She thought then that it was time to make noises about

going. And it was with her anxieties very little lessened by what she had unthinkingly agreed to that ten minutes later she left Doña Eva, having accepted her invitation to come and see her again tomorrow.

The hours until dinner, nine o'clock Juana had said when she had come to her room to deliver her laundry, were spent with Reggie swinging from relief on remembering Doña Eva had said Severo had said he would only marry when he fell in love, to agitated dismay when she recalled the way he had told her that morning that he had paid ten thousand pounds for a bride, and the way he was insisting that that deal was not reneged on.

The weather had changed when, dressed in a deep pink kaftan, she stood at her bedroom window watching the rain tip down outside. She needed to feel she was looking her best, she knew she was looking good—but she found that was all she was sure about, for with Severo Cardenosa she seldom felt very sure about anything. He had the power to confuse, rile and then deflate her better than anyone. Even now she was hesitating between going in search of her temporary fiancé to say her piece before dinner and dithering about whether it would be wiser to wait until they were actually dining. He couldn't very well discover he had something else to do and to disappear if she tackled him while they were eating, could he? And she had to have everything settled tonight, if not to his satisfaction, then at least to hers.

Deciding on the latter course, at five minutes to nine she left her room, butterflies in her tummy, but her face outwardly composed. Her face stayed composed until, turning into the part of the hall where the dining room lay, she saw Severo, dressed in black and looking more good-looking than ever, the material of his suit fitting immaculately over his broad shoulders. He was coming towards her.

'I was about to come looking for you,' he said easily, causing her butterflies to settle a little that at least it looked as though they were going to start off pleasantly.

'Juana told me dinner would be at nine,' she answered vaguely, having to stop when Severo blocked her way and stood looking at her, his glance unhurried as it went from the top of her head and all the way down and back again.

'Am I permitted to tell you you look very beautiful?' He sounded sincere, though she couldn't be sure there wasn't a mocking note in there somewhere.

'Thank you,' she answered politely, and felt her arm taken as he turned about.

Together they went into the dining room, her eyes noting only one end of the table had been laid. Good. She wouldn't have to have a shouted conversation with him had it not been so and a place was laid either end. Conscious that she might need all her tact, mustn't rush into speech which with his seemingly volatile temperament could have him in an instant changing from charming host to snarling aggressor, Reggie allowed him to pull out her chair. She watched while he took his own chair and wondered where she should start. Then she had a few moments' respite when Maria came promptly to serve the first course. Maria's departure had her opening her mouth, but Severo was there first.

'You have enjoyed some of your day?'

He was under no illusions then that she hadn't enjoyed a lot of it!

'I visited your grandmother this afternoon.'

'I know.' Of course he knew; he had most likely spent some time with her when he had finished whatever kept him so busy for most of the day. 'Abuela is very taken with you, Reggie.'

'I—liked—like her.' Now that they had started to talk,

she began to feel better. The time seemed ripe to get this marriage nonsense sorted out.

'I am sorry to have left you so much on your own today,' a tongue in cheek remark if ever she heard one. He had about as much time for her as she had for him! 'But with my presence over the last few weeks being needed at home I have had little time to deal with outside events.'

Without trying, she thought, already losing her way, he had successfully blocked what she had been going to say—and he must have a fairly good idea what was in her mind. Not only that, but he had aroused her sensitivities by reminding her, without actually saying so, that his grandmother too had been through a difficult few weeks, with her husband's health taking a turn for the worse and his subsequent death.

'It must have been a difficult time for all of you,' she said quietly, biting her lip in vexation that from the satisfied look of him he had read that her emotions were at that moment tied up with his grandmother.

It seemed, she thought crossly, that this man was something of an expert when it came to reading people— or was it that her soft heart was so wretchedly visible? She made up her mind there and then to go against her nature. If the only way to deal with this man was to appear hard-hearted, then no one at the Estancia de Cardenosa was going to know she was as soft as butter when her emotions were played upon.

'Tell me, Reggie—I know so little about you—do you ride?'

'You mean horses?'

Really, he was a past master at confusing her! When were they going to get round to the subject that must surely be as much in the forefront of his mind as hers?

Maria arrived to clear the first course and serve the

second while Severo agreed that he had meant could she ride a horse.

'I've been on one a time or two,' she answered; no point in pretending she was brilliant—she wasn't.

'I thought, weather permitting, you might like to come with me to see something of the countryside tomorrow morning.'

The idea appealed, she couldn't say it didn't. If the countryside was anything like what she had seen this morning then she knew she was in for a treat.

'I'd like that,' she said, and found, to her annoyance, that she was smiling into brilliantly blue eyes. Really, the man could charm the heart of a wheelbarrow, she thought, feeling cross again, and determined as Maria went out that she had delayed long enough.

'Your meal is to your liking? I can instruct Maria to prepare only English meals for you if you prefer.'

'My meal is fine, fine,' said Reggie quickly, barely noticing what she was eating, so anxious was she becoming. 'Look, Severo, we have to talk. To talk about—about us—about this wedding thing.'

Deliberately, she thought, he took his time in replying, delaying his answer by pouring them both a glass of wine. He raised his glass to her before sampling from it, then, returning his glass to the table, he suddenly looked directly into her troubled eyes, taking in the vulnerability of her mouth, his eyes lingering on her lips.

'Very well,' he said at last, 'we shall discuss—us.' And not waiting to hear what she had to say on the subject, he continued, 'You were—surprised—were you not, to learn this morning that your sister had—forgotten—to give you that very important piece of information.'

Shocked was a nearer description of how she had felt, but, 'Yes,' she agreed quietly.

'Did you really think, Reggie, that for ten thousand

pounds all she had to do was to come to my home, pretend to be engaged to me and just enjoy an extended holiday?'

Her eyes fell to her plate. She hadn't thought about the money side of it too much at all, she could see that now. But again he was going on before she could answer, a tightness coming to his voice that she didn't care for as he asked:

'Did your sister pass the money over to you as well as the role you are to play?'

Anger rose quickly at the implication that it was his money she was after by coming here. 'No, no, she didn't,' she answered hotly. 'Had Bella not already spent your wretched money it would have been returned to you and there would have been no need for me to come at all.'

'Contract null and void,' he commented. 'A pity for you that your sister had such expensive tastes.'

'The money wasn't frittered away,' she was quick to defend Bella. Too quick she saw a moment later when she had added heatedly, 'Your money went as the deposit on the house she and James are buying.'

'Ah,' he said, so softly, damn his eyes, she just knew she had given him further ammunition to use at a later date. Oh Lord, how easily he could make her lose her temper, make her say all manner of things without thinking.

'Anyway, all that is beside the point, isn't it? My purpose in coming here was to settle Bella's debt to you by playing the part of your fiancée. That I will do. You'll have no cause to complain there, I'll . . .'

'Was it your *only* purpose?'

Quietly spoken, the words reached her. And her anger threatened to erupt again if he thought she was here after bigger pickings.

'What *exactly* do you mean by *only*?' Her own tone was quiet; she was not sure the dining room wouldn't look a wreck if he said just one word indicating that she too was after his money. She'd have to throw something at him, she just knew it.

'Did you not tell me this morning,' he jibed, 'that you love another?' His jibing tone fell away, and as she looked at him, startled that for some hours now she had so far forgotten Clive's existence as not to have thought of him at all, he went on, 'If you love this man as you claim you do, why then are you here in Uruguay and not with him?'

'That's no concern of yours!'

'I think it is. If I am to make you my bride in three weeks, I insist on knowing everything about this man you think you are in love with.'

'I don't think,' she snapped, 'I know I'm in love with Clive.'

The hard glint she had seen in his eyes was there again as she repeated she was in love with another man. But this time she wasn't allowing him to have the next word.

'And you and I are not going to be married in three weeks' time or ever,' she raced on furiously, 'and you damn well know we're not!' One eyebrow ascended as though to tell her he knew no such thing, and afraid he might yet again beat her to it, she rushed on, 'Doña Eva told me this afternoon that you'd told your grandfather you would only marry when you fell in love—so since you have little liking for me, let alone love, that's that, isn't it?'

She felt quite triumphant at having got all that out without interruption. But with that way he had of coolly deflating her, her feeling of triumph was shortlived.

'It would appear neither of us is entering this marriage with love in our hearts for each other,' he told her sardonically. 'But marriage it will be, make no mistake about that, Regina Barrington!' Then, with a coldness descending with a swiftness she found bewildering, he returned to the subject of Clive. 'Your lover obviously has no plans to marry you himself, otherwise you wouldn't be here now. What went wrong—couldn't he bring himself to make that final commitment?'

'Final commitment?' She was playing for time, trying to get her thoughts together, because Severo was adept at scattering her wits.

'He must have loved you too,' he went on, though why he should think it must be automatic for Clive to love her in return, she didn't know. 'Wouldn't he marry you, Reggie, or——' a shrewd look coming to him, 'couldn't he?'

She didn't know why she was hanging back, he'd go on at her until he found out anyway. But her stubbornness wasn't going to let her tell him anything.

'Ah,' he said when she didn't answer. 'Did he feed you the old line—he was married but his wife wouldn't divorce him?'

'She wouldn't.' The words left her hotly, had her gasping as soon as they were out that in her defence of Clive she had confirmed what he wanted to know.

There was no satisfaction in his look as his glance flicked over her. She knew she had gone pink, but it was more, she realised, from the fact that she had told him she loved a married man than from anything else. Had she really considered living with Clive? She saw now that her inner self would have been most unhappy with that state of affairs.

'You met her?'

Clearly he didn't think Clive was married. 'Yes, I met her,' she said woodenly, the scene only too vivid in her mind. 'She came to see me the day Clive once again asked her to divorce him.'

'So he was serious about you? What does he think of

your leaving London to come here?' His voice sharpened. 'I take it he does know?'

'No, he doesn't.'

Her anger had disappeared a few minutes ago; now she only felt dull and lifeless. She had swung round from not wanting to tell him anything to seeing no reason why she shouldn't tell him everything. Perhaps when he knew she had been afraid had she seen Clive again, that, even married as he was and with two young children, she might have still ended up living with him, Severo Cardenosa might well think then that she was not a suitable person to be his bride, mistress of the Estancia de Cardenosa.

'Clive had to go abroad for his firm. Before he went he asked me to consider going to live with him. I didn't know up until then that he was married,' pride had her confessing that in spite of herself. 'The next night his wife came to see me. They have two young children I didn't know about either. That same night your telephone call came through. I didn't understand your call, of course, but when I told Bella about it she was—upset . . .' What an understatement that was! 'Bella knew how I felt about Clive, knew that even knowing he was married, had children, feeling as I did about him then even the beliefs of my upbringing would go for nothing if I saw him again . . .' She stopped there, but Severo qualified:

'You were afraid you would go against the teachings of your grandparents and go and live with him as his wife.'

'Yes.'

'Whose idea was it that you should come to Uruguay?'

Suspecting she might be falling into a trap, though unable to see one, she hesitated, then told him truthfully: 'Bella's.'

'She really was panicky, wasn't she?' was all he said, then, tersely, 'You were lovers, you and this—Clive?' and in case she didn't understand the question, though she understood it all right and was furious at his nerve, 'You were bed partners?'

'That's none of your business,' she snapped. The cheek of the man!

'So you were.'

Let him think what he liked, she fumed stubbornly. Why should she deny it? It seemed to her then that it would give her the edge if he did believe it. Perhaps now that he knew the sort of female she was he would drop this ridiculous idea of them getting married.

Conversation ceased when Maria came again into the room, enquiring of Reggie if she had enjoyed her main course. Reggie looked down at her plate and was amazed to see she had cleared it without the vaguest memory of having tasted anything.

'It was delicious, Maria,' she told her in Spanish.

Her dessert placed before her, the door once more closed behind Maria, she wanted to get back to the subject of the marriage.

'So you see, Severo, aside from any other consideration, I'm really not at all the sort of girl any Cardenosa would like to take for a wife.'

'Why do you say that?'

Reggie dropped her spoon and stared at him in amazement. 'Surely what I've just told you makes you see I'm not a fit person to bear the Cardenosa name?' It hurt her pride to say that last bit, but it was the truth as she saw it.

Her answer was an amused laugh, the first sound of humour she had heard since coming into this room, though she couldn't see anything very funny in what she had said.

'My dear Reggie,' he said smoothly, his laughter dying but his face still showing amusement, 'you aren't the first girl to fall in love with a married man. On your own admission you neither knew he was married or that he had children.' His amused look faded as he said gruffly, 'Nor, in this day and age, are you the first girl to lose her virginity without the benefit of a marriage ceremony. And as for your doubts as to whether or not you would have set up house with this man,' he shrugged, 'we shall never know, shall we?'

'Never know . . . You mean you still intend that we shall—be married?' Reggie was struggling and ready to grasp at anything to get her out of this mess. 'What about—about the money? Aren't you afraid that once married to you I won't try and take you for every penny you've got? I would have a hold on you then, wouldn't I?'

About a minute passed with him giving her a narrow-eyed, stern scrutiny, the seconds taking so long to tick away that with each one she was growing more and more convinced she had won. Women in Uruguay were fully emancipated, it therefore followed that half of everything that was his would be hers. She allowed herself a half smile, certain now that she had scuttled all his plans for their taking a trip up the aisle. Severo would not risk any money-grubbing schemer taking half of what he had worked hard for.

His eyes went to her mouth, observed the small smile lurking there, and then as she watched, an answering smile tugged at his mouth, and his eyes were positively alight when he at last answered, his voice pure silk.

'Sometimes in this life, little Reggie, one has to take a gamble. Had you known more about my countrymen, *querida*, you would know that above most things, the Uruguayan loves a gamble.'

'You mean . . .' Her voice was husky, she didn't want to believe what her brain was telling her.

'I mean, sweet Regina, that I shall take the risk. I intend to marry you on the twenty-fourth of this month.

So now I think you had better start getting used to the idea.'

He had spoken quietly, but what he had said triggered off a violent reaction. Pushing her chair back, she was on her feet, her eyes flashing, only wishing the table wasn't between them so she could wipe that oh, so confident look off his face.

'I shall not marry you,' she said, striving for calm. 'I didn't come here to do so, and—and I have no intention of doing so. I'm sorry to have to hurt your grandmother—you know already that I like her. But you'll just have to think up some other story to tell her. You . . .'

'You really are the most bossy of females,' Severo interrupted, seeming unaware of the short rein she had on her fury. That, or enjoying the way her eyes sparked almost navy in her fury.

'*Me* bossy?' Reggie yelled. 'Why, you . . .' She grabbed at a frail strand of control, and said defiantly, with no intention of going back on it, 'I'm telling you now, Severo Cardenosa, that I am not marrying you, that my decision is final; and that there is absolutely nothing you can do about it.'

'A pity.' His face showed all the regret in the world— but his eyes showed none.

'Pity?' she echoed, feeling an ominous thread of threat just from looking into those blue, unregretful eyes.

He sighed, then smiled pleasantly. 'Perhaps I had better leave it a day or two before I write to James Usher—you did say that was the name of Bella's husband, didn't you?' And while Reggie could only pale and look at him aghast, he added thoughtfully, 'I am sure any letter sent care of your sister will be forwarded from her old address, just as I am sure James Usher would love to know who paid the deposit on his house.'

'You swine!' tore from her throat, and not trusting herself not to empty apricot flan and icecream all over his head, she stormed from the room, wondering half hysterically in her fury if there would ever come a time when she sat down to a meal with him and remained to finish up the last course.

CHAPTER SEVEN

STILL fuming against Severo Cardenosa when she awoke, surprised to find she had slept so well after storming from the dining room, Reggie saw the sun was bright, drying up rain that had fallen last night.

Well, if he thought she was going riding with him he had another think coming! Cutting off her nose it might be, for being a country-lover she had a yen to see more of the surrounding countryside. But honour bound as she was to play his fiancée to the full, she could quite well achieve that without the need to put up with him outside the house as well as in.

A tap on her door heralded Juana's arrival with a tray of tea. Shyly the girl approached, handing her a note from off the tray.

'*Gracias*, Juana,' Reggie smiled, quickly scanning the note to discover that her not so beloved fiancé would be riding in half an hour if she would care to accompany him.

Purely for Juana's benefit, who if her swooning expression was anything to go by assumed Severo had sent a love note, she allowed a smile to hover. Bending to her handbag beside the bed, she took out her pen, musing that she should notch up a mark, since he hadn't come to deliver his message personally, that it must have got through to him that his presence in her bedroom was not required. She turned the note over, intending to write something rude on the back.

It was Juana, still with that look on her face, almost sighing with the romance of it all, that had her checking her impulse. Not that her reply would get into wrong hands—and who else was likely to read English except Doña Eva—but . . . No, she was here to play his fiancée, she would give him no cause to complain he wasn't getting value for his money.

A satirical whim took her and she penned, 'Darling, you overwhelm me—I still haven't recovered from last night.' Nor would she in a hurry!

She was in no hurry to leave her room either, and it was forty-five minutes later, when, sure Severo had gone out, she breakfasted, then wondered what she should do. Returning to her room, she wrote a long and cheerful letter to Bella. Suspecting that James might share Bella's mail at this early stage in their marriage, she was careful not to give any hint of how things truly were, saying she had taken a trip into the interior and liked it so much she was staying there for some weeks. She had no need to hold back when it came to describing the scene she had seen by the stream yesterday, and sealed the envelope knowing Bella would breathe a sigh of relief that apparently her younger sister was experiencing no problems.

She went in search of someone to tell her where to post her letter, still trying to come to terms with the hurt she felt at Bella's deception. That she could let her come all this way, knowing she had deliberately lied in saying Severo had agreed to her coming when he had known absolutely nothing about it, was staggering, but that Bella could so conveniently 'forget' to tell her she had agreed to marry him she found more than hard to take.

Maria did her best to give Reggie directions to a post box, but either her translatory cogs hadn't woken up with her that morning or Maria was going too fast, because they ended up in a dreadful muddle, both seeing the funny side when Maria, a shade desperately, gave up and held out her hand for the letter, saying something Reggie was able to translate.

'I post,' she said.

Reggie handed her letter over, grinning, while Maria's ample bosom moved in unison with her laughter.

Feeling the need to be outside, Reggie collected her sunglasses and was soon in glorious sunshine, her feet unhesitatingly making for the belt of trees at the bottom of the hill, hope in her heart that the same magic she had experienced yesterday would still be there.

It was. The perfume from the wild rose caught her senses. Worries, never far from her mind, bolted. There was no room in this idyllic spot for the recurring perplexed thought of how she was to get out of going through with this marriage; to fret that she hadn't had chance to disguise her butter-soft heart—Severo had seen how much Bella's happiness meant to her and was playing on that for all he was worth.

Losing all sense of time, Reggie stood in the shade of the trees, her eyes feasting afresh, becoming fascinated by a bee busily at work, totally absorbed. The sudden arrival, and departure, of a dove, fitting for the peaceful scene, disturbed yet added to the magic. She followed the direction the bird had flown, not hurrying, finding new delights as she walked beside the stream.

She must have walked about half a mile when suddenly, in the middle of nowhere, the thought not entering her head that someone else might appreciate the beauty too, she stumbled upon a woman of about thirty seated before an easel and canvas, brush in hand. The way the woman turned her head, a frown at the intrusion creasing her brow, told her her appearance was something the artist could well do without.

'I'm sorry,' the apology came automatically and in English. 'I didn't know . . .' Realising the woman wouldn't understand her, Reggie was about to apologise in her halting Spanish, when the frown left the woman's face and she stood up, changing the paintbrush to her left hand and carelessly wiping her paint-smeared right hand down her jeans.

'You are Severo's fiancée,' she beamed.

'Er—yes, I . . .'

'Carlota Mendoza,' the woman introduced herself, her hand coming out, a smile of such friendliness on her face Reggie just had to reciprocate, her own hand coming out to shake hands, 'though everybody calls me Lola.'

'My friends call me Reggie,' she offered, feeling her hand warmly taken, Severo back with her as she recalled that she had once told him that. 'I'm sorry to have interrupted you. I didn't expect to . . .'

'That is quite all right. I was just thinking I had done enough for today.'

Her command of English was so good, Reggie felt quite ashamed of her lack of fluency in Spanish, and felt guilty too that the artist—and from what she could see of her painting, she was very good—should pack her things away on account of her. But Lola, as she insisted Reggie call her, was at pains to assure her she really had been about to finish, adding that she was something of a coffee addict and felt the need for a cup.

'Perhaps you would care to come to my home and share coffee with me?' she invited. 'It is not far.'

Having taken to Lola, and with the invitation sounding so genuine, Reggie thought there was nothing she would like better.

Together they carried Lola's equipment and crossed

the stream by a sturdy footbridge, going over a field and to where several houses came into sight, Lola explaining, on hearing Reggie had done very little exploring so far, that this was where the village proper began.

'Francisco, my husband, he is—er—overseer, I think you call it, for Severo. We have this end house here. The other houses in the village are for people who mostly work for Severo too.'

They went through a gate to the house, flowers in glorious colour, wallflowers and pansies flanking the path, tall hollyhocks standing guard at the front door. Lola complained that when Reggie commented on how magnificently everything grew, that unfortunately, so did the weeds.

Reggie spent an hour with Lola, and the time simply flew as instant empathy flowed between the two. It was from Lola she learned more of Uruguay—when admiring a painting of a matador in full regalia, she learned that Lola had painted it from a drawing for Francisco. Bullfighting, Lola said, was abolished in Uruguay over fifty years ago, though there was still a bullring to be seen at Colonia. From there, conversation easy, Lola acquainted her with the fact that of the country's three million population nearly half lived in or near Montevideo. How they could when the interior was so beautiful amazed Reggie, and having said so and hearing that Lola shared her view, she felt her spirits lift to have found a friend.

But they dipped when Lola mentioned that she had attended Severo's grandfather's funeral, and had spoken with Doña Eva, who had seemed at that time to be at death's door herself.

'But,' said Lola softly, 'Doña Eva has a strong heart,' Reggie took her to mean will, 'and I know how much she was looking forward to your arrival. Your wedding day will put fresh life into her. Have you set the date yet?'

'The twenty-fourth of this month,' was out before Reggie could stop it, and she could have groaned at her stupidity. Now there were two people to be told the wedding had been called off. More, possibly, because Lola was certain to mention it to her husband, and she couldn't very well tell her it was a secret with the date less than three weeks away. And anyway, with Lola looking so absolutely delighted with the news, if she wasn't to let Severo down—though why that should bother her she didn't know—she thought she had better show some enthusiasm. And then she looked at her watch.

'Good heavens, it's gone twelve!' she exclaimed, feeling dreadful that she had taken up so much of Lola's time when she had only meant to stay for a cup of coffee.

'Time does fly when you are compatible with someone,' Lola observed, making Reggie feel a whole lot better at the sincerity of the other girl's tone.

She stood up, saying she had better get back to the *estancia* and apologising if her visit had delayed Lola in preparing her husband's lunch.

'Oh, Franco doesn't often come home to lunch. They feed very well on *asada*.'

'*Asada?*'

Reggie's curiosity delayed her further while Lola explained that it was a type of barbecue where a whole beast was roasted, every scrap eaten.

'Everything?'

'Except the hide. Stay and have lunch with me, Reggie,' Lola further invited.

But Reggie had to excuse herself. 'Maria will have cooked something for me, I think,' she refused regretfully, only then the thought came that she had forgotten to tell anyone where she was going. 'I'd better get back—er—Severo might come home to lunch.'

Lola's understanding smile at her last remark was with

her when she crossed back over the little wooden bridge. Not sure how long it would take to get back and mindful that Maria's efforts could be ruined, she hurried on, grateful to keep in the shade of the trees.

On rounding a bend near to the place she had dubbed as her spot, she stopped short. For there on the very ground she had stood to look her fill earlier was the most splendid-looking stallion she had ever seen, its coat entirely black, and astride him the man she had sent that satirical note that morning. Watching for her, waiting for her, she knew it. The look on his face was not at all pleased.

For the moment she was too stunned by the sudden vision of horse and rider—they seemed so well matched as to appear one—standing there in her spot, just as though Severo had known that that was where he would find her. Then a gust of wind, coming so suddenly, and from nowhere, had lifted her skirt waist-high and she was too busy battling to cover the long length of thigh, not to mention the laciness of her briefs that Severo couldn't avoid having a full view of.

As suddenly as it had sprung up, the wind died down, but not so her colour. She moved forward, pink in her cheeks telling of her embarrassment when, closer, she looked up at Severo. The displeased look had left him, she saw, and in its place was the most devilish grin she had ever seen.

'Perhaps I should have warned you about the *pampero*, *darling*,' he had received her note, then, 'a south-west wind that springs up unexpectedly. Its consequences have been known to sweeten the sourest feelings in any man's heart.'

Undoubtedly he had been feeling sour because she had disobeyed his instructions to tell someone where she was going.

'I forgot,' she said simply, lamely. 'I just came out—and I forgot.'

'Maybe you will remember another time,' was all he said, then he reached down a hand, the reason for which she couldn't understand as she looked back at him in puzzlement. 'Don't you want a lift home?' he enlightened her.

On the back of that brute of a horse? 'No, thanks—it's—er—too much for one horse to carry you and me—and besides, it's uphill all the way.'

She turned and had gone perhaps two steps, when her feet left the ground. In one movement she was sitting across the stallion, her back hard against Severo's chest.

She was too frightened initially to make any protest at all. Then Severo had set his steed in motion and she was too busy then being afraid she would fall off and hit moving ground that seemed to be a mile away to make any protest.

But she need not have worried. Severo had no intention of allowing her to fall. For while he had full control of the stallion, mainly from his knees, she thought, his arms were firmly about her waist, the strength and muscle of them vibrating through the thin material of her dress.

As one, the horse with its two riders cantered up the hill. Modesty a thing of the past, Reggie was more intent on staying put than in attempting to cover her knees.

At what point the ride became enjoyable she couldn't have said, but enjoyable it suddenly was. Excitement stirred in her, making her aware of the superb horseman holding her safe, the whipcord strength of him totally reliable. It's only excitement at the unexpectedness of it, she told herself, then forgot everything but the pleasure of having the cooling breeze of movement fan her cheeks, playing tangling games with her hair.

Severo was first off the stallion at the house, his arms coming to assist her down. Those arms were again round her as automatically she clung on to him till her feet touched the ground. Her eyes alight, it didn't seem at all unnatural to stand in the circle of his arms, her face delicately flushed, hair in wild disorder, animosity for the moment forgotten.

'That was super!'

She thought a flame of some kind lit his eyes, and felt the arms about her tighten fractionally, then he had let her go, remarking drolly, 'I enjoyed it too,' causing her to wonder if he had meant he had enjoyed purely the ride or the fact of having her up there so close to him.

It must have been the ride, she thought, relaxing, for he didn't follow up the remark but looked past her to where a bow-legged stable hand was walking up to them.

Handing over the reins to Pancho, Severo turned to her saying he would see her in the dining room in ten minutes. Eleven minutes later, changed from her full-skirted cotton dress into a more fashionable one, Reggie entered the dining room. Severo was already there, she saw; he had showered, if his damp hair was anything to go by, and was now dressed in fawn slacks and a sports shirt.

'Would you care for a sherry?' he asked in the polite manner of the perfect host. It was clear that any remembrance of their closeness atop the stallion not too long ago had been washed from him under the shower. So why couldn't she so easily have washed that remembrance away? It was crazy, she thought, to have her mind dwell on it so much.

'No, thank you,' she answered equally politely, her expression cool.

Throughout the meal Severo conversed with an ease she found very attractive. Any fears she might have nursed that this meal like all others would end in full-fledged flight were not realised as they reached the pudding stage without so much as a cross word coming from either of them.

She could see no point in repeating herself by bringing up her refusal to marry him. It appeared he had no wish to talk of it either, as he asked how she had spent her morning, the only note of tension coming when she said she owed Maria for a stamp.

'I will settle with Maria,' he said, and before she could get out she could afford to pay her own postage, he was asking sharply, 'Who did you write to?'

The sharpness of his tone had her struggling not to retort in kind. 'Not that it's any business of yours,' she replied, only just managing to keep her voice even. Who did he think he was anyway to assume he had a right to know with whom she communicated? 'I wrote to my sister.'

'I trust you sent her my love.'

Sarcastic devil! 'You didn't even get a mention,' she said sweetly. Then she realised things were very close to blowing up, and just at this minute—again she recalled those firm arms about her, and frowned—she didn't want to fight with him. 'After that,' she said, forcing herself to concentrate on what else she had done, 'after that I went for a walk and met Lola Mendoza. I had coffee with her.'

She had earned a good point, apparently, for the tightness left his face. 'You got on well with Lola, by the sound of it.'

'Very well. She's a lovely person, isn't she?'

'She is,' he agreed. 'A fine artist too. Her husband Franco is a first-class overseer. I am fortunate to have him.'

Reggie guessed then that Francisco must be his right-hand man. He must have been a great help to him when because of his grandfather's health Severo had had to remain near the house.

She finished her coffee and stood up. There was nothing now to keep her in his company. He rose too, but when she would have left him with a polite word, he said:

'I think my grandmother would appreciate a visit from you this afternoon, Reggie.'

Desperately trying to think up some reason why she shouldn't go, certain he had not yet acquainted Doña Eva with the news that there was to be no wedding, and unhappy to let the old lady believe there would be a wedding, Reggie could come up with nothing.

'Must I?' she asked.

'It is a long day for her without visitors.'

Oh, he knew how to pull on her heart-strings, didn't he? She gave him a speaking look he received imperturbably, and forgot all about politeness as she flounced out. He knew damn well after his remark that she could do no other than visit his grandmother.

But when she went to visit Doña Eva, despite a mutinous, 'I won't go, I won't!' that attacked her in her room, she found the old lady looking far more frail than she had the previous day. She determined then to keep her visit short so as not to further exhaust her.

The will Lola had spoken of was there strongly as Doña Eva made her welcome, sending Ana to make tea and making every effort to sound more lively than she looked. Her own grandmother had lived only six months after her husband had died, Reggie thought sadly as she answered Abuela's question of was she comfortable in her room. If appearances were anything to go by it didn't look as though this dear old lady had so much as six months in her.

'May I pour?' she offered impulsively when Ana had brought the tray, remembering yesterday the shaky hands that had lifted the silver teapot, and hoping Doña Eva wouldn't think she was being impudent.

'Why, thank you, my dear,' said Doña Eva, settling back in her chair, her snowy white head resting against the support. And when Reggie had placed her cup on the table where she could easily reach it, she went on to enquire if she minded very much giving up her dancing to come to be married to her grandson.

Since Reggie had missed entirely that Severo must have told his grandparents about Bella being a dancer, her brain sped into overdrive before she settled for, 'It was an easy decision,' and saw she had said the right thing. Doña Eva smiled warmly as though to acknowledge that once bowled over by Severo she could understand that nothing else on earth would matter for her but that she be with him.

Shortly after tea was drunk Reggie made her departure, but not before Abuela had her promise that she would again come and take tea with her the next afternoon.

Two days following her meeting with Lola Mendoza, Lola telephoned her asking her to share coffee with her if she was free.

It was in that week that a pattern her days were to follow emerged. During the morning she would walk, discovering more and more of the countryside. Sometimes she would come across Lola, who would insist she go back to her home with her for coffee. Having packed a swimsuit in the hope of perhaps doing a spot of sunbathing, having no idea then that there was a swimming pool at the *estancia*, she would spend part of the afternoon, first making sure Severo was nowhere about, swimming in the pool, before going to shower and dress and then have tea with Doña Eva.

A week later, having just left Doña Eva, she wandered

into the *sala*, her mind heavy with the thought that she seemed to be getting deeper and deeper into the tangle of this marriage business. Doña Eva had casually let out that the wedding cake had been made and was ready for icing. Since Severo had said nothing to Abuela about the wedding being put off to some obscure date in the future Reggie had decided it about time she exerted herself and did it for him. But just looking into those blue eyes so like his, eyes that had known such recent sorrow, she just hadn't had the heart to say anything.

Cowardly, that was what she was being, Reggie fumed against herself as she stared out of the window on a day that was still warm for all it was clouded over. There was nothing for it but that she would have to bring the matter up with Severo again. There had been ample opportunity since they had dined frequently together, but the conversation, pleasant, she realised now, as it had been, had been on purely impersonal matters. He hadn't said a word about marriage since that night she had wanted to empty her pudding over his head. But she could see if she had hoped he had accepted she wasn't going to marry him then with the wedding cake already being made, he had done nothing to stop it—and the twenty-fourth was getting closer and closer.

'How do you feel about showing me what sort of a horsewoman you are?'

Too far away to have heard the subject of her thoughts come into the room, Reggie jerked round to see Severo standing there. He didn't look as though the sight of her in her pretty but simple cotton frock, her blonde hair loose about her shoulders, displeased him, and how long he had been there she had no idea. But since he was the very person she wanted to see, she wasn't going to overlook this opportunity.

'Can you give me a minute to get into some jeans?'

'I'll give you five,' he answered, the charm she had sometimes seen in evidence.

She was almost out of the door before she slowly came to a halt and turned to own, 'I'm not very good.' Charm was replaced by a lift of his left eyebrow, his mocking expression telling her he was all ears to hear the confessions of a non-virgin so that her right palm itched as it had so often since her very first contact with him. Stiffly she added, 'As a horsewoman, I mean,' going on, her back rigid, 'I'm not coming if you have it in mind to put me up on the back of a stallion like the one you were riding the other day.'

'And I thought you enjoyed it,' he mocked.

One of these days, she fumed, pulling on jeans in her room, dragging her hair into a rubber band—just you wait, Severo Cardenosa, one of these days! She recalled one of her grandfather's sayings when she was getting above herself when gaining the upper hand at cribbage. How he made her laugh when he adopted that confiding manner and trotted out, 'Many a little sparrow chirped in the morning—'twas dead before nightfall.'

She frowned as she closed her bedroom door, realising the analogy didn't fit. Grandfather invariably beat her at cribbage and no one, not even his worst enemy, could liken Severo to a sparrow. A hawk maybe, a waiting hawk—was she still the little sparrow her grandfather teased her of being?

To her relief the mount Severo had saddled ready for her when she joined him was a comfortable-looking old thing. His own horse wasn't the stallion either. Whether or not this was because he didn't think that magnificent brute would take kindly to doing no more than a steady trot, Reggie couldn't be sure, though she gave him the benefit of the doubt if he had ridden the stallion hard that morning and was now resting him.

'Come and say hello to Pétalo.' Severo scanned her face, its fine contours visible with her hair pulled back, then impersonally helped her into the saddle. He adjusted her stirrups, satisfying himself as they set off that she at least knew the rudiments of horsemanship.

Aware she knew more than the basics, Reggie would like to have galloped off and left him standing. But since she hadn't been on a horse since she was sixteen—apart from that memorable occasion that wouldn't seem to leave her when she had sat up in front of him—she thought it better for her knowledge to return gradually rather than go showing off and very possibly taking a fall.

Severo took her a way she hadn't ventured before, past corrals that housed some terrifying-looking beasts, telling her he had a programme of very selective breeding; adding to her knowledge that whatever he did there was nothing haphazard about it.

Cantering now that she had her 'sea legs', they travelled over acres of blue-green grasslands, Reggie's own mount being as surefooted as the horse Severo was riding. From time to time they slowed, many of the fields they rode over having wire fencing, all in good order, she thought, as one might expect to find on any well run ranch.

When they came across a herd, thousands of them to her mind, and to her delight all Herefords by the look, a breed she could recognise, one man, dark-haired like Severo and nearly as tall in the saddle, separated himself from the rest and came over, Severo turned to her and introduced Francisco Mendoza.

'Lola's husband!' Reggie exclaimed, delighted to meet him as she extended her hand to the man who had ridden to her side, his own hand coming out.

'I have heard about you much,' Francisco said shyly,

his English good, but not as good as his wife's. 'Lola find happy with you,' he added, which Reggie thought was the nicest compliment.

'I am happy to have Lola for a friend too,' she returned, and meant it. From Lola she had learned so much about Uruguay and its people, of Rodo, author of *Ariel* and *Los Motivos de Proteo*, of Artigas whose statue she had seen in Montevideo, the man who had fought so hard for his country but who had then spent thirty years in poverty and isolation in Paraguay.

Franco she thought a dear of a man, just the right partner for Lola. They spent some minutes with him before wheeling their horses and going once more over rising and falling ground.

When they came to a steep bank, Petal wasn't the only one with the bit between her teeth when Reggie saw that Severo intended they should ride down it. She knew he was watching her every step of the way in case she couldn't handle it, and needed all her concentration. She was concentrating so hard it wasn't until she had raised her head from guiding Petal that she saw Severo had brought her to another of those exquisite little streams she seemed to come across all the time in this department.

'Oh, Severo, it's perfect!' broke from her, for here again were trees, different ones from her own special place, trees of oak and poplars, and shrubs and colour.

'I thought with your eye for beauty you might appreciate it.' Had he brought her here especially to see this spot? she wondered, her hostility towards him mellowing. But before that thought could take root, he was saying, 'We'll rest the horses here. They could do with a drink,' which had her cancelling the thought that he had done anything for her benefit. He had purely seen, where she had not, that the horses were thirsty.

She would like to have dismounted unaided, but firm

strong hands were at her waist—hands that set her free
the moment her feet touched terra firma. When he chose
to lie down on the grass, because she thought now was
perhaps the most ideal time to get a few things off her
chest, Reggie elected to sit down not too very far away
from him.

It was difficult to know where to start. Diplomacy, she
thought, was called for. Lead up to it. She knew he could
turn into a fiery brute if she handled it wrongly. So instead of going right to the heart of the matter she asked
him a question that had been in her mind for a day or
two now.

'Severo . . .' he turned his head her way, his attention
hers. 'You know I often go and have coffee at Lola's
house.' He nodded, his blue eyes watchful. 'Well,' she
plucked a blade of grass, knowing her nerves were more
for what was to come than from any worry as to what his
answer would be, 'well, would it be all right if I asked
Lola up to the *estancia* occasionally so I could give *her*
coffee?'

She had upset him, she could see that even before he
answered. Her spirits dipped as she watched and saw a
stern expression take him. What had she done now?

'I am most surprised to hear you ask that question.'
She was afraid of thunder, yet here was a storm brewing.
Well, she wasn't afraid of him, she thought bravely, and
snapped back,

'You mean you're too much of a snob to want your
overseer's wife taking her ease in your *sala*?'

Immediately she knew she had said the wrong thing.
Fury lit his face, a quick movement as though he was
going to get up and shake the daylights out of her was
checked as his hands clenched, and there was nothing
casual about him at all as he gritted:

'Both Lola and Franco have sat at my table many

times. It is a pleasure to have them in my home. You . . .'

'I'm sorry, Severo, I'm sorry,' she burst in before he could let go on his opinion of her. She had known as soon as the hot words had spurted from her lips that she was wrong, very wrong. The very way she had seen him with Maria, Juana, Pancho, told her there wasn't a snobbish bone in his body. 'I spoke without thinking. I—I think I must be a little on edge.'

Like the *pampero*, as soon as his temper had sprung up, Severo's anger died. He gave her a half smile that made her breathing easier.

'That is perhaps natural in a bride-to-be,' he said softly, and while all her anxiety sprang immediately to life again, he went on before she could get a word in, 'What I meant, and you so obviously misread when I said I was surprised by your question, was that as my future wife you have a right to ask anyone you please into our home. It surprised me that you felt the need to ask such a question.'

Oh, this had gone far enough, far, far enough! 'For the last time, Severo Cardenosa,' she said, having no need to shout because he wasn't very far away, 'I—am—not, repeat *not*—going to marry you.'

Steadily he held her gaze, her words coming through loud and clear. Then coolly, in the manner only he had to rile her so, he sidetracked her and succeeded in sparking off dynamite.

'Had the adulterer Clive been better placed financially no doubt your feminine misgivings about going to live with him would not have got in the way.'

Her gasp was audible before a sheet of red misted her eyes. 'You swine!' she abused him. And beside herself, 'You *insufferable* swine!'

White-hot rage seared all rational thinking. She was on her feet, flying at him, her fury beyond words needing physical assault to assuage it that not only had he dared to defile the love she had for Clive, but that he could think that money mattered where her heart was given.

Unfortunately the few yards that separated them were liberally strewn with potholes, and as the toe of her shoe unerringly found one, she tripped and went sprawling on top of him. But winded as she was, she was so blazingly mad, her fists started flailing just the same—though not for long.

Without effort, it seemed, and she was a wild fiery bundle to contain, Severo had rolled her over until she was beneath him, his well muscled arms having no trouble in anchoring her arms out of harm's way.

And his fury was matching hers when he snarled, 'You little hellcat! *Dios*, I said there was passion in you—perhaps passion of this sort will tame you!'

And while her mouth was all set to heap further abuse on him, his mouth came down on her parted lips. And if Reggie had thought at any time in her life she had been thoroughly kissed, she was just about to learn that she had never left the nursery slopes.

'Let me go!' she raged, infuriated when his lips left hers briefly, her body heaving against his to get away.

'Like hell! Not now I've got you where I want you,' he breathed savagely.

Again his mouth descended, his shoulders now keeping her hands to the ground as his hands came to the back of her. His lips crushing hers had her trying to bite him, but it didn't seem to bother him as he kept the pressure there, making her want to cry out when the only punishment her teeth were making was against her own lips.

'Let me go!' she raged again when he raised his head to look into her furious face.

'I'll teach you to swear at me,' he ground out. 'I already owe you for one slap I was too gentlemanly at the time to collect on.'

'Gentlemanly!' she scorned, 'huh!'

'For every insult offered, *darling*,' he told her, his anger seeming to lose its edge as she arched her body at him in a vain attempt to get away, 'you may be sure I intend to be recompensed.'

'Go to the devil!' she snapped.

'Another insult,' he muttered, and claimed her lips once more, his kiss this time lingering, his mouth less hard as the kiss went on.

It confused her that there was no longer aggression coming through from his mouth to hers. She thought that was what confused her anyway. For when he lifted his head again, she discovered some of the fight had gone out of her. Insults she had ready to hurl at him staying locked up inside. It's only because I know if I insult him he'll insist on kissing me again, she thought, but her eyes were showing her confusion as Severo looked into them and saw the storm in her abating.

Gently this time she felt his lips over hers, and her confusion was complete when she discovered she quite liked the way he was kissing her. Her own mouth softened beneath his. And it was then Severo began to kiss her so that she lost all thought of fighting him. Her lips parted and as his hands at her back moulded her to him, her arms, without her knowing they had been released, were going up and around him.

There was such pleasure to be gained from that mobile mouth that kissed her eyes, her throat, somehow opened the V of her shirt and kissed the rounded mound that swelled away from her bra, that she could only delight in the moment.

His lips came back to hers and as he drained from her, yet lit new fires that had the most abandoned longings starting in her, an awareness of cool hands that had lifted her shirt from her jeans and were now caressing her, nearing her breasts, had an unwanted sanity trying for a hearing.

'Don't,' she moaned, even then wanting to bite her tongue out for having dared to have spoken.

He stilled over her, the hardness of his body warning her, scaring her into knowing she had left her 'don't' too late. Panic found a hold. She couldn't—not with a man who thought her a girl on the make. It was panic that had her body wriggling to be free.

'Be still,' a thickened voice commanded. 'Your provocative, gyrating body is clouding my thinking.'

Instantly she did as she was ordered. If he was still capable of thinking then perhaps he wasn't so far gone as she had thought.

Then suddenly she was free. He rolled away from her to sit with his arms on his knees. For long moments he said nothing, and realising the closeness of her escape Reggie was in no mind to remind him of her presence.

Then swiftly he looked at her and she wished he hadn't. Her hair must look a mess, the rubber band could be anywhere, and she hadn't got a comb with her. Her cheeks, from the way they were burning, just had to be rosy, and remembering the way her arms had held him to her, she had never felt so embarrassed in her life.

'At least,' said Severo, himself enough for that mocking note to have survived, 'at least you will arrive back at the *estancia* looking as though there are some parts of this engagement that give you joy.' He then stood up to go to the horses, 'We will start back now. Abuela will be joining us tonight—dinner will be early.'

CHAPTER EIGHT

It wasn't fair. It just wasn't fair, Reggie fumed, seated at the dinner table and wishing she could be hard enough to take that smiling look from Doña Eva's face.

It hadn't bothered her to find they were to be four at dinner, not three as she had supposed. The portly gentleman somewhere in his late fifties had been introduced as Señor Felipe Armaral, but as dinner progressed it soon became apparent that he was a minister of religion. Worse, Doña Eva brought the conversation round to the wedding, and it was obvious that Señor Amaral was to conduct the ceremony.

Glancing at Doña Eva, she saw she looked happier than she had seen her, the subject under discussion bringing life to her face. But she still looked frail and delicate in her pale blue dress, Reggie saw, and knew she didn't stand the remotest chance of getting to her feet and denying there was to be a wedding.

And Severo knew it! He had told her Doña Eva would be at dinner, but deliberately hadn't told her who else would be present, *or* his calling. He knew very well she would suspect something and have a word or two to say on the matter.

She caught him looking at her and threw him a look that should have shrivelled him, but drew only a bland smile that had her hanging grimly on to her recently awakened ear-boxing tendencies.

Sanity had come back once they had ridden from where that passionate interlude had taken place. Fool that she was, she had thought better then than to return to the sole reason she had gone with him in the first place.

'More wine, *querida*?'

She came out of her reverie to refuse politely, 'No, thank you, darling,' oh, so sweetly. 'I think I've just about had enough for one day.'

'The night is yet young,' he had the last word, as he turned to refill Señor Amaral's glass.

'Two o'clock for the wedding will be much better than the morning,' Doña Eva addressed her, reasoning, 'If it turns out to be a very hot day then the guests will miss the noonday sun and will be better able to enjoy the party in the garden afterwards.'

Reggie found herself agreeing that two o'clock was an admirable time for the ceremony, when what she really wanted to do was to jump on the table and scream that there wasn't going to be any wedding. It was no consolation to tell herself that it wasn't that she didn't have the guts to do such a thing, but that despite Doña Eva seeming so much better tonight, she still looked frail—how could she be the one to cause even the slightest setback to her health?

Very shortly after dinner Doña Eva gave a delicate little yawn, whereupon Severo immediately teased her into confessing that she did feel a little tired. It was then that Señor Amaral asked if they would mind if he took his leave, his parting remark being that it wouldn't be long now before the two of them stood in front of him.

Rebellion hit Reggie as soon as she was alone, and nothing would have kept her there to wait for Severo to return from seeing his grandmother to her rooms. Smartly she went along to her own room, fuming afresh as she washed and changed into her nightdress. It was all his fault. He knew exactly how she felt about this marriage business—she had told him plainly enough only this afternoon. Remembering the afternoon triggered off other thoughts. Thoughts about her own astonishing behaviour. Aroused thoughts of the unbelievably passionate being that had lurked unknown inside her. The feeling Severo had disturbed, brought to life . . .

Rapidly, as though to escape from thoughts she didn't want to dwell on, she jumped into bed, concentrating only on the thought that it was all Severo's fault. At any time during the evening he could have put an end to the marriage conversation, the arrangements. But no—had he? Not on your life. If anything he had spurred on such talk.

True, *she* could have said something; fairness gave her a nudge. But how could she? She recalled the sweetness of Doña Eva's face and knew she was learning to love her as she had her own grandmother. She would have done anything for Gran—just as Severo was endeavouring to do all he could for his Abuela. He was ready to go through with this marriage to save her from knowing the happiness her husband had known at the last was gained from nothing but terrible lies.

For hours, or so it seemed, Reggie lay awake trying to oust the ferreting of her thoughts and find sleep. But in the end she had to admit defeat. She got out of bed wide awake, her brain alive with all that was going through it.

Hot, bothered and bewildered, she shrugged into her cotton housecoat, knowing if there was to be any chance of sleep for her that night, then first she was going to have to sort herself out.

Noiselessly she left her room, and was still pacing up and down the verandah some fifteen minutes later, her mind nowhere at peace. Thoughts of Bella and James had crowded in to add to her confusion. Their chance of happiness would be in tatters if she didn't give in to Severo; he had made that very plain. Yet strangely, as her thoughts leapfrogged on to Doña Eva, it was thoughts of that kindly lady that gave her the greatest compunction. A sigh escaped her as she saw again Doña Eva's face as she had bidden her goodnight. There had been love in that tired face for the girl she thought would soon be her granddaughter by marriage.

Doña Eva's face swam before her, her own growing affection for the old lady smiting her. She remembered the teatime sessions they had spent together, Doña Eva not holding back, treating her like one of the family. Oh, how could she be the cause of adding to the grief she was already going through? It would be like spurning that ready love that was there for her—like stabbing Doña Eva in the back.

And suddenly, a ton weight lifting, Reggie knew she couldn't hurt her. At last she knew what she was going to do. She turned, ready now to go back to her room, her decision made. Perhaps now she might get some sleep.

A figure coming out of the shadows had her stifling a squeak of alarm. But even in the darkness she knew that tall figure. 'How long have you been there?' she demanded, not at all happy that if he had been there any length of time, he couldn't have avoided witnessing her pacing up and down as she wrestled with her conscience.

'Not too long,'' was the obscure reply as he came up to her. 'The beauty of the night drew you out of bed, did it?' he asked suavely.

She bit down hard one or two not very polite names she would have called him. Beautiful night it was, the dark sky lit by numberless stars, but she didn't doubt he knew full well what was keeping sleep from her.

Unspeaking, she stood about a foot away from him, saw a firefly dart by, and realised then that since he was not making any attempt at conversation he had guessed the mental ferment that had been with her since that first morning at the *estancia* had come to a head—the floor was hers.

Tension suddenly sprang up between them. She could feel it, almost touch it. And for all Severo's outline looked as cool and relaxed as ever, she knew he felt the tension too.

She opened her mouth, and it was out, her first intimation that she was likely to back down from her shouted, 'I am not, repeat *not* going to marry you!' of this afternoon. 'If I marry you . . .' That was all he waited to hear.

In a movement he had taken her arm and was escorting her into the garden, away from the house. Admidst the fragrant smell of night-scented stocks where they couldn't be overheard, he dropped her arm, deliberately trying to rile her, she thought, by prompting:

'You were saying—when we marry . . .'

'I was saying *if* I marry you,' she answered tightly, determined to let him know she was in charge of the 'if', though privately conceding that he had a stack of aces in his hand. 'Then—then how—long will I have to stay married to you?'

'Waiting for Clive?' His voice was sardonic in the darkness.

That did it. That really did it. Why did he have to keep bringing Clive's name into it? Reggie wished she had never told him about Clive. She turned, ready to storm indoors. If Severo was going to carry on in his sweet sarcastic way then he could talk to himself!

Severo's hand caught her arm before she had taken more than a step. She halted, took a few deep breaths, conceding he was right. Running away would settle nothing. Far better to have this discussion now, then live through every day as it came, including her wedding day, until such time as she could get away and fly home to England.

'I apologise for my remark.' His apology was as un-expected as was the hint of charm that came through with it that asked forgiveness. She could imagine him using such a manner as a child and getting away with murder.

'That's all right,' she found herself saying, and tried not to get uptight again that it looked as though she was another sucker for his charm.

'You were asking for how long our marriage would last.' His voice was deadly serious now, sombre she would have said, when he added, 'You have seen for yourself the state of Abuela's health.'

Reggie sobered too, an ache in her heart for Doña Eva. The old lady had looked quite spritely tonight—but so had her own grandmother on occasions towards the end, nagged a little voice.

'I know it sounds terrible,' she said quietly, 'b-but are we agreed that when—when anything happens to Doña Eva, then I'm free to leave?'

'What makes you think I should want you to stay?'

The cold, insolent question had her anger threatening, until she realised how very painful it must be to him, who had so loved his grandfather and lost him, to now be having this cold-blooded discussion of his grandmother's passing.

'I'm sorry,' she apologised, when it was he who was at fault. Then, striving to be businesslike, for that was all this was to Severo, a business transaction, she asked, 'You will divorce me at the proper time?' This was a pre-dominantly Roman Catholic country, she didn't want to wake up one day and find she had tied herself to him for life.

'Divorce in Uruguay presents no problems,' he answered, going on to inform her, 'We must thank José Batlle y Ordoñez, the great reformer, for that. Not only did he ensure that women have equal rights, he also made divorce easy for them—women do not even have to give cause of why they wish for a divorce.'

She was relieved to hear it, and to her mind that just about settled everything. She was about to go in when something else occurred to her, and was out before she could dress it up.

'One other thing—this marriage,' and having started she had to go on, 'Well, I mean—nothing like—like what happened this afternoon will—er—happen, will it?'

'You are suggesting I cannot wait to get you into bed?'

That mocking note was back. But this time she wasn't going to storm off until she had the answer she wanted. Though if he followed up and said, 'I thought you enjoyed it,' the way he had about her ride on the stallion, she didn't give her temper any great chance of being held down.

'Will it?' she demanded between her teeth, holding on tightly.

As though the idea of him ever wanting her as his bed partner was something that amused him, he covered his laughter with a sigh, and misquoted, 'Always the best man, never the groom.' Then as she stubbornly refused to budge until he had answered properly, he said, 'For ten thousand a man might expect a little—er—home comfort, but I can just as easily play away from home.'

Irritated by his reference to the money, irked to know he thought her no better than Bella where money was concerned—though that was the first time she admitted Bella had a less loveable side to have taken the money at all—over the top of that, Reggie discovered she didn't like at all that Severo could so openly intimate that when it came to other women, marriage wouldn't restrict him at all.

She started to walk back to the house, wanting to shrug

his hand away when it came to guide her as the name Señora Gomez, not heard in over a week, shot into her head. She nearly did pull away, but a picture of herself in an undignified heap if she fell over, a distinct possibility in the darkness, had her allowing his hand to stay on her arm. He could go to his other woman, why should she care?

But once on the verandah thoughts of the unseen woman who had had him dropping everything to go with her on that day of her arrival had her tugging herself free. She would have gone to her room then without another word had Severo not instructed:

'Be sure to change into another nightdress before you go to bed, *querida*.'

'What?' she was startled into asking.

'It is a dewy night. The hem of your night attire will be more than a little damp.'

In her room Reggie was silently fuming. Even in the darkness had he missed nothing of what she was wearing? It was of no help to see the hem of her nightdress was soaked.

The click of her bedroom door had her eyes coming open, realisation waking with her that with so much on her mind she had certainly slept well. Then the noise that had awakened her had her sitting up, the shoulder frill of her nightdress slipping down one arm.

'Good morning, *querida*.' Coolly Severo came away from the door and before she could order him out, 'Good, I see you took my advice.'

'Advice?' She wasn't fully awake yet and she blinked, followed his eyes and saw he was appreciating the top half of her in her fine covering. 'How did you know that . . .' she broke off, realising he couldn't possibly know she had changed her nightdress, but that she had just confirmed it for him. Her lips firmed as his grin got to her.

Hurriedly she righted her frilly shoulder strap, dragging the covers up past her bosom, thinking resignedly that she had as much chance of ordering him out and him actually leaving before he had said what he had come to say as she had of being an astronaut.

Without wasting further time, he came and sat down on the edge of her bed, dipping his hand into the jacket pocket of the suit he was wearing, then handed her a bundle of notes.

'What's this?' Pride was to the fore, determining that whatever was in his mind she wasn't touching a single penny.

'It occurred to me, since your sister forgot to give you all the details, that it is more than possible you have nothing to wear on the twenty-fourth.'

Reggie hadn't got round yet to thinking about a wedding dress, but she realised now, for appearances' sake if nothing else, she would need a dress that wouldn't let the Estancia de Cardenosa down. From the talk at the dinner table last night it appeared that as well as family friends, every gaucho Severo employed, plus wife and children, would be attending this noteworthy date in the history of Cerros de Cielo.

Reluctance was written all over her as she looked at the money, and saw hopelessly that she was going to have to take it. He was the piper. But in trying to overcome her pride her voice came far more snappy than she had meant as she aimed for some of his sarcasm.

'What do you suggest I buy—something sweet and innocent in white?'

'Perhaps grey would be a more suitable shade.' Had she hoped for an understanding of her dust-bitten pride, then there was nothing but hardness there, as he slammed into her, 'We both know Clive took from you the right to wear white—or wasn't he the first?' She was still wincing from the unfairness of his remarks, gall rising, when he commanded, 'Get dressed, I'll take you into town.'

'Go to hell!' she flared, determined to buy black, black, black. 'I'll go with Lola.' Then she shrank back. Severo was on his feet looking ready to throttle her.

'*Dios!* One of these days, Regina Barrington,' he threatened, seeming to be keeping his distance with difficulty, 'one of these days I shall take great pleasure in settling with you.' You and whose army? she wanted to retort, but didn't dare, he looked so flaming. 'If Lola's car is out of action I damn well *will* take you!'

He was determined one way or another that she was to be kitted out then, Reggie fumed, as the door slammed after him. But once she was washed and dressed her determination to wear black faded. Apart from her promise to Doña Eva, she just didn't think she had the nerve.

Lola, in the middle of washing when telephoned, was thrilled at the idea of going on a shopping expedition, saying her temperamental car was behaving beautifully at the moment, but her washing machine was playing up. 'I shall have to wait for it to finish now I've started. I'll pick you up in about an hour.'

Reggie insisted she would walk down, their friendship having progressed so that Lola agreed, laughing, 'Come now—you can make us an early coffee while I finish off.'

Grinning herself, Reggie felt more lighthearted for having spoken to Lola. Having selected her most comfortable sandals, she picked up her bag and went outside.

The Volvo parked on the drive was one she had not seen before, vehicles of callers to the *estancia* ranging from bicycles and motorbikes to other makes of car. But it was the slim dark-haired woman standing not far away in conversation with Severo who drew most of her interest. She looked to be in her thirties, was elegant, and—as a

dart of unrecognised emotion pricked—to her mind pro-
prietorial, if the way she was hanging on to Severo's arm
was anything to go by.

For appearances' sake Reggie couldn't ignore Severo.
No one must guess at what they really felt for each other.
Though oddly, at that moment Reggie would have been
hard put to it to define what emotion he did arouse in
her.

'I'm just off, darling,' she addressed his back, for some
reason wanting to break up what the woman was so ear-
nestly saying to him.

The dark-haired woman, beautiful, she saw, up close,
though not liking her hard eyes, looked startled at the
interruption, and Reggie's lips tightened that whatever
was going on, the woman didn't have the grace to remove
her hand from Severo's arm when she must know Reggie
was his fiancée.

Just at that moment Severo turned. Reggie admitted
her interruption was rude and out of character, but from
the speculative look in his eyes she wondered if she had
straightened her face fast enough. He had once accused
her of being jealous—laughable idea—but that narrowing of his eyes told her something was going on behind
the smile that suddenly appeared.

'You haven't met Manuela have you *querida*?'

He knew damn well she hadn't. He'd been keeping her
tucked away, hadn't he? Reggie's thoughts were mutinous as she went through the motions expected of her.
Manuela Gomez's handshake was of the limp lettuce var-
iety, though she too, by the look of her, had been properly brought up and said how delighted she was to meet
Reggie at last, being too much needed at home to get
over too frequently.

'But Jorge, my husband,' she explained, 'and I
wouldn't miss your wedding for anything.'

Soon after Reggie excused herself, walking quickly down the drive, Severo's, 'Don't overtire yourself, *querida*,' ringing in her ears. The idea that the two were having an affair took root, refusing to move. Manuela Gomez had been all over him!

Oh, she had been right to suspect something was going on. Just who did they think they were fooling? She had seen that secret look Manuela had given him when it had seemed he was about to offer her a lift to Lola's. Manuela had been quick to butt in, 'If we could get back to my place as soon as . . .' She hadn't had to finish, Severo's soothing, 'Of course, Manuela,' told Reggie her appearance was an unwanted intrusion. Jorge, she decided, poor sap, must be out for the day. No woman would be so blatant as to take her lover into her home when her husband was there. Though remembering Manuela Gomez's hard eyes, she wouldn't put that past her.

As ever in Lola's company Reggie cheered up, and the twenty miles to the nearest town of any size were soon covered. Lola knew where to begin their search and was helpful in suggesting, when Reggie saw a rather nice short dress, that perhaps a long one might be better. She saw then that Lola knew exactly what was expected of a Cardenosa bride, and went along with her suggestions. This whole day was more for Doña Eva's benefit than her own anyway, so why not?

She hadn't got so far as thinking about a veil, but when Lola spotted the most exquisite mantilla of fine lace, it was then that she dug her heels in. It seemed to her that almost from the moment she had set foot on Uruguayan soil she had lost sight of her own identity. That all the blame for that could be lain at Severo's door was indisputable, for until she had met him she hadn't been aware of having this short-tempered streak in her, this demon anger that had her regularly itching to take a swipe at him. Before coming here she had always been totally in control of her person—admitted, there was a certain weakness where Clive was concerned, but never, ever had she felt like hitting him. Even when he had told her he was married she had taken it without anger. She was numbed, stunned, she supposed, and dragged her mind back to Lola who was still singing the praises of the mantilla.

'I—er——' The last thing she wanted to do was to upset her friend, but if she had to go through with this wedding—and what other choice was there?—then suddenly, with a determination that wouldn't falter, she knew she wanted some part of her own identity in there somewhere. She was an English girl after all, not Uruguayan. 'I rather fancied the sort of veil I would be wearing if I was being married at home.'

Straightaway Lola was on her side. 'Of course you do,' she said, giving her arm a light squeeze to show she wasn't offended that the mantilla she so much admired was being rejected, apologetic herself for not thinking, and was in rapid conversation with the sales assistant, who spoke no English, before Reggie could draw another breath.

They were both tired at the end of their expedition. Lola insisted on driving Reggie up to the *estancia* but refused her earnest invitation to come in for refreshment.

'Some other time,' Lola apologised. 'I'd better get back and tidy up a bit before Franco comes home.'

Reggie stayed on the drive to wave her away, her tiredness lifting as she thought of Severo's face when he saw her in her demure and innocent white complete with veil. Hugging her purchases to her with something akin to glee, she went to her room and was soon visited by Juana asking if there was any service she could do for her.

'Nothing, thank you, Juana,' Reggie told her in her

slow Spanish, and the idea sprang into her head that it might give Doña Eva a lift to see her wedding dress, though she wondered at the feeling inside herself that said she just had to show her purchases to somebody, 'I think I'll go and talk to Doña Eva.'

'Good, you're back,' Doña Eva greeted her warmly when Ana had shown Reggie, complete with parcels, into her quarters, and having already taken her own tea she instructed Ana to make some fresh. 'I expect you could do with a cup. Severo told me you'd gone shopping with Lola.'

'I'm gasping,' Reggie smiled. 'But what I really came for was to show you my wedding dress.'

Doña Eva's face was expressive as Reggie shook out the fine white matt material of her dress, her approval evident as she exclaimed at the tiny white silk roses that decorated neck, hem, waist and cuffs. But when Reggie showed her her veil there were tears in the old lady's eyes, happy tears as she related that her own veil had been very similar.

Ana too came to admire, and talk about the wedding went on for some minutes, with Reggie for the first time feeling able to enter into the spirit of the thing since now she had agreed to go through with it she had no cause to think all this talk was for nothing.

Her dress carefully folded in its carrier and Ana once more about her duties, Reggie, sitting in her usual seat beside Abuela, was suddenly alarmed to hear her state that she would be leaving for her own home on the day of the wedding.

'But you can't!' Apart from the fact that she was growing dear to her, she felt horrified that there would only be her and Severo once Doña Eva left.

Doña Eva patted her hand gently. 'It's nice to know you want me in your home, Reggie, but it wouldn't be right. It's not right that you start your married life with a member of your husband's family in residence.'

'But . . .' Reggie began to protest.

'Yes, I know I have my own apartment and you need never see me if you don't wish to. But with Severo saying you're not going away on honeymoon—your own business, I'm sure, for all I find it most peculiar—I don't wish to be here so that on your honeymoon at home, when you'll be wanting to spend all your time together, you'll feel you have to come along to see me.'

Reggie took her parcels back to her room, not liking at all this turn of events. But as the days wore on and, the day of the wedding came nearer, she began to adjust to the fact there would not be many more afternoon visits to Abuela. And thinking about it deeply, she came to the conclusion that miss seeing her as she would, perhaps it was just as well. She had seen Maria in conversation with Ana a time or two, and who knew, with Maria's garrulous tongue, unquestionably loyal to the household as she was, she might well pass on to Ana, who was also a limb of the household that for a honeymoon it was most peculiar that the new mistress slept alone in her room.

That part of the whole proceedings worried her from time to time. Severo had his pride in full measure and she wasn't lacking either in that department, but to have the staff discussing their night-time activities—or lack of them—was something that was abhorrent to her. Still, she sighed, remembering personal pride had been out in force on both sides when Severo had refused to take back the change from her wedding dress, expensive as it had been, abhorrent or not, it was something she just couldn't bring herself to discuss with him. Three times this week she had eaten dinner alone, and she didn't care if she was getting crabby in her old age that she took such great pleasure from hoping that Manuela Gomez's cook was not a patch on Maria.

The day before her wedding she gave serious thought to whether she should write and tell Bella, for James' benefit, that she had met the most divine Uruguayan, Severo Cardenosa, and was marrying him. She decided against it. She could tell her sister she had gone through with the marriage she had 'forgotten' to tell her about when she was back in England, the marriage annulled.

Her wedding day dawned as beautiful as any young bride could wish. But as far as Reggie was concerned it might just as well have been raining cats and dogs. Severo had chosen the same time yesterday as her to visit Abuela. He listened as she had done while Doña Eva said they mustn't see each other before the ceremony tomorrow, and heard his grandmother remark that she thought she looked a little pale.

'Excitement, I expect.' His eyes had given her a thorough going over, his voice, purely for his grandmother's ears, she knew, was surprisingly gentle as he asked, 'Are you feeling quite well, *querida*?'

Nerves about the whole of the next day were the cause of her paleness, she knew. For from what she could make out the world and his wife would be in attendance. Severo would take being the centre of attraction in his stride, but the idea of her being the centre of attraction too, and to so many people, literally terrified her. But an unexpected imp of devilment had taken hold of her.

'Oh, wouldn't it be just too awful if after all these preparations I was ill and it had to be cancelled?'

'We'll get you to the church, my darling,' said Severo, 'if we have to take you there on a stretcher.'

With Abuela looking quite blissful that Severo would stand no obstacle in his impatience to make her his bride, Reggie had done her best to look as if it was the loveliest thing she had ever heard—a tough assignment, when she could have thumped him for the threat she alone knew was behind his words.

Because there were so many visitors to the *estancia*, it being decreed she would be worn out with entertaining before she got to the church, Reggie had a luncheon tray brought to her room. She was not hungry, but because she knew she was going to need all her strength for the reception afterwards, she forced as much of the meal down as she could manage.

The morning had ticked by with dreadful slowness, jitters setting in so that she had to force herself to remember that Bella's debt had to be paid, hope in her heart that there wasn't anything else Bella had 'forgotten' to tell her.

If the morning had dragged, then once her tray had been removed the time simply flew. Juana's big moment too had arrived. She was all shyness and smiles as she helped the girl who would soon be mistress of the Estancia de Cardenosa into her bridal finery.

Then Reggie was leaving her room, Franco Mendosa escorting her to the charming village church. The church was full to overflowing. She gripped on to Franco's arm as if seeking a lifeline, last-minute panicky thoughts of, this is wrong, all wrong, taking her.

And then she saw Severo, his attire formal, a friend from his university days standing with him. And she knew then, pride in every line of the back to her, as much for his sake as for his grandmother's, that in front of all these people who respected him, she couldn't let him down. She couldn't take to her heels and run, and keep on running.

Franco took her to the man with whom she was to be joined in a loveless marriage, and as Severo turned, all thought ceased, nothing remembered until she came out of church as his wife. For those brilliantly blue eyes held a proud admiration she had never expected to see, and as she looked back through her misty veil, she could only wonder that his eyes took on a brief warmth especially for her.

She was able to reason, as she stood with him hoping her smile would hold up as professional and amateur photographers alike clicked away, that any special warmth she had seen in him must be because everything was going as planned.

The reception, expertly catered for, was not the ordeal she had had nightmares about. Severo kept by her side for most of the time and she was grateful for his support. There was no way she was going to remember the names that went with every hand she shook, though the face of Jorge Gomez, Manuela's husband, a man about twenty years older than his wife, did register. Never had Reggie seen a more worried-looking man. He was of stocky build, but with a pride in his bearing she found endearing, that pride making him momentarily drop his anxious expression for a smile as he congratulated Severo on his beautiful bride.

'I thank you for your congratulations, Jorge,' Severo replied, turning his blue eyes on her, her veil now away from her face, 'and I agree—my bride is beautiful.'

For an age afterwards, even when people had eaten their fill, old and young alike getting up to dance their own interpretation of the music coming from an immaculate-looking sextet, Reggie could not get the worried face of Jorge Gomez from her mind. She just had to wonder if he knew about the affair Severo was having with Manuela, her feelings most unbridelike towards her new husband if that was what had put that defeated look there.

The celebrations were almost at an end when she had the answer. No, he did not know. Severo had seldom left her, but standing with Lola and Franco, she saw him talking to Manuela's husband, nothing hostile showing. If anything Jorge Gomez appeared to have a lot of time for Severo, and listened hard to anything he had to say.

Since it couldn't be what was going on between him

and Manuela that they were discussing, Reggie decided since Uruguayans were so proud of their democracy then most likely they must be talking politics, though the main political parties, Blancos and Colorados, were still much of a mystery to her.

Perhaps because Jorge Gomez had looked happier leaving than when he had come, Reggie was feeling better disposed towards Severo when the last guest had gone. So it wasn't so much of an act when he said, 'Abuela went to her rooms a few hours ago, as you know, but now I think she will want to start her journey home. Will you come with me to say goodbye to her?' to genuinely agree that it was unthinkable that Doña Eva should leave without her first seeing her.

'Your grandfather would have been so proud this day, Severo,' Abuela said as they walked with her and Ana to the waiting car, one of the men from her own household having come to drive them home.

Doña Eva then turned, her thin arms embracing her granddaughter-in-law, and having learned that her grandparents had completed her upbringing:

'And your grandparents would have been proud of you too, my dear,' she said softly, and while Reggie was fighting against tears, she added, 'But this too for me has been one of the happiest days of my life. I thank God that I'm alive to see it.'

She then kissed Reggie before turning to kiss her grandson, who handed her into the car, tucking her skirts around her before he leaned to kiss her cheek.

Reggie's eyes were brimming over as she stood on the drive with Severo waving at the car. Then, knowing he wouldn't understand, she turned, intending to hurry into the house.

Only she didn't make it. Severo's hand, fast on her arm, was turning her, so she just had to face him. Relentless fingers beneath her chin forced her head up, making her look at him.

Tears glinted on her lashes and she wanted to pull away. 'Ah, *querida*, do not look so sad,' he said gently, and while still holding on to her he bent and kissed first one cheek and then the other. 'Today Abuela is happy, is she not? Do not waste your tears on sad thoughts.' And then, as though determined to cheer her up, 'Come with me, I have something to show you.'

'I'd better go and change out of my dress, hadn't I?' she asked, mesmerised for the moment by his charm.

'No,' he said decisively. 'What better way to see your wedding present than dressed the way you are?'

'Wedding present . . .?'

But already Severo was taking her over the drive and to where the outbuildings and garages were.

CHAPTER NINE

OPEN-MOUTHED, unable to find words, Reggie gazed at the little red Mini that was Severo's wedding gift to her.

'I never expected . . .' she found her voice, surprise evident. 'What made you . . . I haven't got anything for you.' And as she recalled that she had told him at that first meeting she had had to sell her old car to pay her air fare, embarrassment rose. 'You shouldn't have done it, Severo—I never asked you for anything.'

Instantly she knew she had said the wrong thing. He looked annoyed to be reminded of his opinion of her, his opinion that she was out for anything she could get. Then as though determined that today at least would end without them firing broadsides at each other, he suddenly grinned, putting his arm across her shoulders when he noticed as she had that Pancho too had come to look at the car.

'It is expected of me to give you a wedding present, *querida*,' he told her, his glance flicking to Pancho.

Oh, so that was it! The staff would no doubt wonder what gift the master had given his bride. Why she should feel let down that the Mini, no inexpensive item, had been given purely to satisfy his inquisitive work force, she couldn't have said, but it reminded her that she still had a part to play.

'It's a lovely gift, thank you, Severo,' she said politely, and keeping brightness to the fore as he turned her towards the house, 'Have I time to change and try her out before dinner?'

'I'll come with you,' was her answer as they crossed the verandah and into the hall.

Was he coming with her in order that the staff should see he couldn't bear to let her out of his sight? Or was it just so that he could check on what sort of a driver she was before he let her loose on her own?

Any delving into the answer didn't get under way. For his arm had remained about her shoulders, and making to leave him where the hall branched to her room, she found him guiding her in another direction.

'What . . .' she began.

Smoothly, not faltering in his step, forcing her to go with him, calmly he told her, 'The room you were using is no longer fitting for the bride of Cardenosa.'

Don't panic, don't panic. Try and be as calm as he's sounding, she told her fluttering nerves, recalling that Maria had told her that first evening that Severo had instructed that the best room at the *estancia* be prepared for her. Yet here he was announcing that the room was no longer fitting for her!

When he stopped outside a door, then pushed the door open, she couldn't have said what her thoughts were. He stood back to allow her to go forward, following her into a room that seemed everywhere to be draped in white.

White bedcover, white curtains, even a tremendous arrangement of white flowers stood in a vase on the dressing table. Without saying a word, trying with everything in her not to be aware of him standing watching her, Reggie went to the whitewood wardrobe, opening doors, to see, as she had been beginning to suspect, that her clothes had at some time during the day been transferred from her old room.

Still unspeaking, she closed the wardrobe door, her nerves taut as she saw from the corner of her eye the casual way Severo had propped himself up against the wall to let her get on with her inspection. There were two other doors in the room. It was as she spotted them that the tension that had been mounting in her started to ease.

The first door revealed a bathroom, white also. Trying not to hurry and thereby betray the anxiety Severo probably knew was threatening to have her in a state of collapse, Reggie opened the other door.

Relief roared in so that she very nearly collapsed anyway. It was another bedroom. The thoughts she had had about the staff speculating on the distance between their two bedrooms must have visited Severo too, she realised. And she saw, too, that this way, giving her a room that adjoined his, though perhaps slightly thought-provoking to have separate rooms, could be taken by the staff to be some modern idea they both shared.

Looking on both sides of the door, she hoped for some signs of a key, a lock, but there was none. Then, recalling how Severo had avoided them having a fight by cooling the situation out by the car when he had looked annoyed with her, she determined she wasn't going to start a fight

either, and spoke for what must be the first time in all of
five minutes.

'I'm not too happy,' she began, her voice breaking off
when he straightened from the wall looking ready to top
any comment she made, 'about the—er—habit you have
of coming into my room without knocking.'

Her anger flared briefly when he burst out laughing,
then died. And she had to turn away because ridiculously
she felt she wanted to laugh too, that she had come out
with what she had when he must have been expecting her
to blow her top.

'You are wonderful, Regina Cardenosa,' he told her,
amusement still in his voice. Because she hadn't screamed
and yelled at him? Or because he could see she didn't like
it, but knew exactly why he had moved her to this room?
'Are you afraid I shall come in one time and find you in
the—altogether?' Amusement was still there, but Reggie
no longer felt like laughing and it showed. 'Will you feel
better if I give you my word that I will always knock
when I find it—imperative—to see you?'

Was he being sarcastic? She gave him a solemn stare
just in case. Then as though that was the end of the discussion, and she wasn't sure then whether or not she had
his word he would first knock before coming in, he said:

'Change as quickly as you can. You ate very little at
the reception and must be hungry. We will drive for only
a very short distance.'

She did feel hungry when they returned from putting
the Mini through its paces. It was a delight to her to be
behind the wheel of a car again—a car this time that
didn't have the temperamental bent of the one she had
sold.

Back in her room, changing from the jeans she had
hastily donned, she felt she had needed that short spin in
the car. The pricked balloon feeling that had her sagging

when Severo had left her room was now a thing of the past. She had that day been married, but apart from changing her name, her room, very little else had altered.

At dinner Severo was at his most charming, not once saying anything guaranteed to have her firing up. And with Maria twittering in and out from time to time, her look softening each time it fell on her, Reggie knew that especially tonight she had to be on her best behaviour.

When the meal ended and with Severo being so charming, she found she was able to say without embarrassment, 'It's been a long day. I think I'll go to bed.'

'It has been a long day, as you say. I don't think I shall be so very far behind you,' he agreed pleasantly. 'Would you like me to send Juana to you?'

She remembered Juana's dreamy romantic expression of that morning. 'No—no, thanks.' Severo rose to escort her to the door, and suddenly she was nervous, though she knew she had no cause. 'G-goodnight,' she stammered before he barely had the door open, and without waiting for his reply, she bolted.

In her bath she calmed down. What an idiot she was! There had been nothing in his manner to cause her alarm, but she had raced away from him like a scalded cat.

The bath water was relaxing, causing her to stay luxuriating in its scented vapours longer than she might have normally. But at last she let the water out, gave her teeth a final clean and in cotton housecoat and nightdress she opened the bathroom door.

And then all the fears and alarms she hadn't permitted to surface were there in full number. For there, only a robe covering him if his bare legs and naked throat were anything to go by, stretched full length on top of her bed, lay Severo.

Words came before thought, rocketing from her on a

tide of fear. 'Get out!' she yelled.

'A delightful way to greet your new husband,' he drawled, getting up from the bed and coming to stand at the end of it.

'I—I . . . you . . .' she spluttered.

'I did knock,' he mocked, and when shock seemed to have her spellbound, he gave her a highly amused look, then took a flat parcel from the bed she had been too blind to see. 'I merely came to give you this.'

Warily she approached, not taking her eyes off him. 'What is it?' she asked distrustfully.

'It won't bite, that's for sure.' Thrusting the parcel into her hands, he watched while Reggie slowly undid the wrapping while keeping a weather eye on him.

It was a picture, a painting of her own private place down by the stream, its beauty captured so perfectly she was numbed by it. Her fears, whatever they had been, vanished as she just looked and looked at it.

'Oh, Severo!' was all she was capable of breathing, her voice, soft and weepy, telling him of her emotion. 'Why?' quietly found its way from her.

'Why?' He paused, then said gently. 'Because I wanted to give you something more personal to you than the car.'

'Why?' she asked again, puzzled, and saw him shrug.

'Call it my thank-you for the way you have been with Abuela.'

'I don't need thanks for that—I've grown fond of her,' she said, her voice taking an edge that Severos thought she had to be rewarded for the small comfort she had been able to give Doña Eva.

'I know,' he said quietly, and that made her feel a whole lot better that for the first time he was showing he believed without question anything she told him.

'It's beautiful!' Her eyes were again on her picture.

'I got Lola to paint it for you.'

'You did?'

Reggie was overcome suddenly that for days now Lola had been busily at work on her picture without her knowing it. Her emotions were haywire that a week or more ago Severo must have gone to Lola and asked her to do the painting, must have taken her to her spot to show her exactly what he wanted, then sworn her to secrecy. That coming on top of a day when she had had to watch every time she looked at him so no one should know there was no love lost between them, was suddenly too much, and her emotion of the moment, the lovely picture in her hand, got out of control.

'Thank you, Severo,' she said, and quite without thought reached up and kissed him.

Then she had cause to wonder what she had done, for Severo's face showed he didn't like her action one little bit. Or so she thought as he looked back at her recently scrubbed face, her brushed and shining blonde hair, for he had taken hold of both her arms and was pushing her away. Already she was regretting her impulse, before he let her know in no uncertain terms that her foolishly given light kiss was in danger of exploding a highly volatile situation.

'*Dios!*' snarled from him. Then he was demanding harshly, 'Do you *want* this marriage consummated?'

Her sharply voiced, 'No!' was accompanied by the slamming of the communicating door.

Finally, not without shedding a few tears, Reggie at last fell asleep, to wake early the next morning with the memory of Severo slamming out last night waking with her. Then, barely before she had time to rumple the other side of the big double bed, something she had decided for the look of the thing she must do every morning, Juana was there, coming shyly in with her tea.

There was only one cup on the tray, she observed, but

her wonderings of would they expect her to be alone every morning were cut short by Juana saying shyly that Don Severo had said not to disturb her if her mistress was not awake.

Reggie drank her tea, her eyes going to the painting standing on a chest of drawers, quelling any softening towards Severo for the thoughtfulness of his gift that he had known how much would please her. He had known the delight she had taken in that particular spot. She decided not to think about him, and set her mind instead on thinking she must thank Lola for the work and artistry she had put in. Though it would look a little odd if she called on her today—the first day of her honeymoon. She made up her mind to telephone her later. But how to fill in the rest of her day?

That problem was taken care of when Severo found her in the breakfast room. Determined to be civilised to start the day at least, Reggie was the first to speak.

'Good morning.'

His night's sleep didn't seem to have improved his temper at all, she thought, as he grunted a reply. He helped himself to a cup of coffee, giving her a chance of a better look at him without being observed. She thought he looked as though he hadn't slept very much at all. Then abruptly he looked up, and caught her looking at him. Quickly she dropped her eyes and concentrated on spreading marmalade on toast. Severo had something on his mind, she was sure of it.

There had been a brooding look on his face anyway; she hadn't missed that. Well, if he was about to tell her not to go flinging her arms about him and kissing him again, he needn't bother, she was thinking mutinously, when his voice broke into the stillness of the room, and what he had to say had nothing at all to do with her action of last night.

'Since we have done away with a honeymoon, I have decided it will be better if I stay near the *estancia* this week.'

Raising her eyes from her plate, Reggie wondered if he woke as a grouch every morning, but kept her face politely interested for whatever else was coming—though she had to agree that for the look of the thing it would be better if he gave the appearance of being unable to drag himself away from her side.

'Yes, I understand that,' she commented quietly.

'Good. I shall take the day off. We will go riding.'

'That will be nice.'

Really, she thought, as her agreement to his order—it was hardly a request—was received in stony unamused silence a moment before he strode from the room, his coffee untouched as though she had turned the milk sour, though peering into his cup she saw he took it black; really, I can see I'm in for a whale of a fun time!

But contrary to her expectations, over the next few days, when she and Severo went everywhere together, they weren't getting on too badly at all. They were both on their best behaviour, of course; Severo knew as well as she did how quickly they could flare up at each other. But it was three days now and not once had they had a row. Several times, now she came to think of it, he had actually made her laugh, had joined in her laughter and looked for the briefest of moments as though seeing her laugh pleased him.

Well, he wouldn't want her to go around with a long face would he, she thought as she walked to her favourite place, for once alone since someone from the next department, Tacuarembó, who had not heard Severo was on his honeymoon, had called on a business matter.

She stood silently in her beautiful surroundings, never bored with her view, and was lost in silent contemplation until a scurrying sound had her eyes turning to where an armadillo was hurrying to a place in some bushes.

Seeing the armadillo brought back a memory of a song she had sung at school, the words partly forgotten. Quietly she began to hum the song she thought had been called *Rolling down to Rio*, then as words began to come back to her, she started to sing, 'I've never seen a jaguar, nor yet an arm-a-a-dillo, billowing,' or was it dillowing? What the heck was dillowing? She laughed unselfconsciously and sang on regardless, 'dillowing in his armour, and I s'pose I ne-e-ever will. Ye-et weekly from Southampton,' her voice took strength, 'gre-at steamers white and go-old go-o rolling down to Rio, go-o rolling down to . . .'

Her voice came to a sudden stop. Where had Severo come from? She hadn't heard him. Yet there he was, standing stock still and looking at her.

'You sound happy,' he remarked softly, then, 'Are you happy, Reggie?'

She hadn't thought about it. By rights, with things as they stood, she should be downright unhappy. But, to her bewilderment, she wasn't.

'Do you know, I rather think I am,' she replied in wonder.

And her spirits didn't sink down to her boots when Severo put an arm about her, for there was no one to see, and said, 'For your honesty, I will escort you back to the house and you can have a whole bottle of Coca-Cola to yourself.'

She didn't mind Severo's teasing, she discovered, her embarrassment at having been caught warbling her head off was quickly got over with him in this mood. But she tried for sobriety as they walked back up the hill.

'Has your visitor left?' she asked.

'We don't want any interruptions in this time of getting to know each other, do we?'

It was an answer she hadn't been expecting, and she had no idea how to reply. If it was still part of his teasing then he wouldn't thank her for taking him seriously. But if he was serious, then what on earth did he mean by it?

At the house Juana greeted them with a letter that had come for Reggie while she had been out. Severo took the envelope addressed to Miss R. Barrington from Juana before Reggie could move, studying it as he escorted her to the *sala*. His look was deadly serious now as he handed it over. Then without a word he went out.

Having given her enough time to read her letter in private, he returned some minutes later, the tray of refreshment he was carrying saying where he had been. But on seeing the shaken expression on her face, instead of offering her a tall glass of refreshing liquid, he deposited the tray, then promptly came to sit beside her on the couch.

'What is wrong? Your sister is ill?'

Reggie blinked, trying to pull herself together. Her letter wasn't from Bella but Clive. And it wasn't so much what was in his letter that had left her shaken, though at one time the contents would have had her overjoyed, but the fact that seeing his name at the end, realising she had barely thought of him recently—difficult though that was to believe—unshakeably she knew she no longer loved him.

At that point, impatient to know what the letter contained since she looked too shocked to answer him, Severo, before she could stop him, had taken it from her and begun to read. Begun to read, one glance at the signature having his mouth going in a tight line, that Clive, distracted to find her flat closed, had gone to see Bella and James. James was off sick with a tummy bug and Bella was out shopping; James had found the letter Reggie had sent Bella and given him her address. He had been flabbergasted to learn she was in South America, but would she come home quickly because he loved her very much, and the greatest news—Irene had agreed to divorce him.

Knowing Severo wouldn't hand over her letter until it was all read, Reggie sat watching, his face far from teasing now as, hard-eyed, he continued down the page to where Clive had written that he would soon be free to marry her.

As he came to the end he stood up, words not needed to tell her the camaraderie they had shared these last three days was over.

'So,' he said, looking down his arrogant nose from his lofty height, his features chiseled in unapproachability, 'the beloved Clive will soon be free to make an honest woman of you.'

'I . . .' she tried, but Severo just wasn't interested in anything she had to say. Not that she was too sure what she wanted to tell him anyway, other than that she saw no reason why he should be so coldly furious.

'No doubt you will be writing back to your lover explaining that unfortunately you yourself are married. Perhaps you would be good enough to give him this message from me. He may not give a second thought to breaking any of the vows he makes, but Cardenosa will *never* break his.'

The door closing quietly behind him told her of the mighty control he was exercising. His fury had been tangible almost—but why? Surely he didn't have such a low opinion of her that he thought she would rush to Clive on the first plane out!

He thought she was in love with Clive, though, remember, she pulled herself up, still finding it difficult to believe that that was no longer the case. How could one fall out of love so easily? Hers wasn't a fickle nature. Yet at one time she had been afraid her love for Clive might have her ending up living with him. Did that mean she had never truly loved him? Perhaps it did, she thought, trying to make sense of her confused thoughts. Had she truly loved him would she have hesitated?

She shook her head as if hoping to clear it, saw the jug of iced orange and, needing a drink, poured herself a glass, sipping as she tried to make some sense of her thoughts. For a long time she sat there, and the ice in the jug had long since melted before she had sorted everything out.

She could never truly have loved Clive, she had realised, not in the way someone should love the person they were going to spend the rest of their life with. She had told Severo only a short time ago that she was happy, and she had been—proving she didn't love Clive—for how could she be happy so far away from him had she loved him? And that day she had responded so wildly to Severo's lovemaking—she should have known then that she didn't love Clive, because had she done so everything within her would have fought at having another man's arms around her.

Reggie left the *sala* to go to sit in her room, instinct telling her Severo wouldn't come looking for her. She hadn't liked his cold fury at all, and she only hoped he had got over it when next she saw him. Why he had been so angry was obvious, since it mattered a great deal to him that his grandmother's remaining days were to be spent as tranquilly as possible. He wouldn't stand for her being upset should his wife leave him before they had been married a week.

That he had coldly told her to tell Clive from him that he would never break his vows—meaning, she supposed, that he would never divorce her—surprisingly didn't distress her. Coldly angry though he had been, she took it it had been said in the heat of the moment. And to her further surprise, she found a little glow starting inside when it dawned on her, if she had got it right, that Severo might have come to like her a little since the implication that he thought Clive was the sort to jump in and out of marriage willy-nilly could mean that Severo wouldn't want to see her hurt when it came to her turn.

Perhaps I'm being fanciful, she thought later that night, selecting her very best dinner gown to wear. Perhaps Severo didn't like her at all. There had been no liking in his face back there in the *sala*. But as she showered and dressed that little glow wouldn't disappear, and she had too much else on her mind to wonder why it should please her to think Severo liked her a little.

But the idea that he had any liking for her soon came to grief when she walked into the dining room at the usual time. He was already there, but his terse greeting soon told her she was his least favourite person. Even for Maria's benefit he wouldn't put on an act. But when from behind his shoulder, serving the second course, very much aware that the honeymooners must have had a tiff, Maria looked at her, her face so comical as she gave an expressive shrug of her shoulders as though to say, 'What's up with him?' as unhappy as she was now feeling, Reggie just had to grin.

'You find something funny?'

He might have waited until Maria had gone from the room before he rounded on her, Reggie thought, as Maria, reading from his tone that battle stations had been sounded, hurried from the room.

'No, I . . .'

'Perhaps now that you have heard from your lover,' his tone was biting, 'now that you think it will be roses all the way, we shall have to suffer you going around with that idiotic expression on your face. Well, allow me to tell you . . .'

But Reggie was allowing him nothing. Cut to the quick by his biting sarcasm, stirred to fury herself, she was on her feet. 'You can go to hell, Severo Cardenosa—the sooner the better!'

She would have stormed from the dining room then, but she never got as far as the door. For he was there before her, lifting her almost bodily to push her ungently down into the seat she had so rapidly risen from.

'As my wife you will obey the courtesies befitting you,' he told her harshly. 'You will stay and eat your dinner and not let Maria nor any of the staff know that since the receipt of your lover's letter you cannot bear to be in the same room with me.'

'I . . .' she began, wanting to tell him that nobody but he could possibly know what was in her letter, and that Clive had never been her lover, not in the way he thought, anyway. But she stopped, her own fury getting the better of her that just as if she was some recalcitrant schoolgirl he was making her stay to finish her meal. 'Oh, you're impossible!' she snapped instead, picking up her hastily tossed aside napkin.

'And you,' he snarled, 'are bloody impossible!'

And on that sweet note Maria was unwise enough to come in again.

'I'll ring when I want you,' Severo told her shortly.

Reggie ate, simply because it was the quickest way of getting away from the morose man across from her. And when the last crumb was finished, determined not to be cowed by him or any other man, she offered a sweetly sarcastic, 'Please may I leave the table?' and received the blackest of looks for her trouble.

Because it was such a hot night, she showered again before donning a fresh nightdress and getting into bed. Usually she covered herself up to go to sleep, but it was so close, she lay on top of the bed, her thoughts of Severo

not at all pleasant as she ruminated on what she would like to
do to him. And he had the nerve to say she was impossible!

She heard him come to his room, checked the luminous
dial on her watch beside her and saw it had gone midnight and hoped he would have the same trouble getting
to sleep that she was having. Why should he sleep the
sleep of the easy conscience after the way he had been to
her?

At last she did fall asleep, but not for long. Had she
known the weather pattern of the country better, known
about the *tormenta*, a localised thunderstorm, she would
not have fallen asleep at all.

The night had been unusually hot, and it was the
rumble of thunder that disturbed her, its dying roll still
audible as she came fully awake. And disappearing with
the sound went all memory of what she would like to do
to the man she had married.

Lightning forked vividly in the sky, and her stomach
knotted up in tension as she jerked upright waiting for the
thunder to follow. It followed almost at once, making her
fingers fly to her ears, and her heart thudded as she tried
not to cry out.

Again lightning lit the sky. Lit the whole room, thunder—crashing so loud it was impossible to shut out—hard
on its heels. Reggie's mouth went dry, all thought ceas-
ing, as fear consumed her as she huddled in the centre of
the bed.

Oh God, I can't stand it, she thought, as thunder came
again, cracking with a violence of such force as she had
never heard before, Lightning chased it so that she was
unsure which came first. Then both came together—the
blinding light, the ear-splitting crash. It was right overhead and she wanted to scream in panic. The lifeless faces
of her parents haunted her, that memory brought vividly
to life.

How many minutes she sat petrified, the storm, the rain lashing the windows, fighting to handle it by herself, she couldn't have said. But when another flash came, making her gasp for breath in her fear, everything around appearing fluorescent, she just couldn't take any more. Like lightning herself she was off the bed, streaking for the communicating door, careless that Severo might throw her out, might still be the cruel, heartless person she had left in the dining room. Thunder, and the door was open. She was through it, calling his name in her terrible fear.

Lightning speared light into the room, her sucked-in breath leaving in a scream. She had a brief moment to see Severo sit up in bed, but in the silence that followed the thunder was too overwrought to hear anything he had to say, but she was pouring out:

'I'm frightened—oh, Severo, I'm so frightened! Please—p-please let me stay with you.'

Lightning lit the room again. She saw his lips move but heard not a word. She saw only that he had pulled the bed sheet back from the other half of the double bed, and as thunder continued in the most deafening racket overhead, she needed no second invitation to hurl herself across the room to the bed and into his arms, barely aware that he hadn't rejected her.

'I can't help it,' she cried when the noise abated temporarily, clinging to him, unaware that only her thin nightdress separated them and nudity. She was completely in the grip of her fear as she babbled out the way her parents had died, the fact that she had been in the car with them, and her fear of thunderstorms ever since.

Severo cradled her for long, long minutes, his voice soothing, his touch on her bare arm as he stroked her in comforting movements quieting when thunder, not sounding so loud now, came again. But thunder was still about and Reggie was terrified the storm might return.

'Will—will it come back again?' she asked tremulously, her fear apparent though rhyme and reason were trying to get a footing.

'It may, *querida*,' he told her quietly, continuing to stroke her with one hand, his other arm about her trembling shoulders. 'It does sometimes.'

'Oh?' escaped fearfully, then she was suddenly aware of him where before she hadn't been. 'I'm—I'm sorry,' she stammered, conscious of that movement of his hand on her arm, his arm around her. Knowledge came, when she discovered she had her arms around him, that it was a warm muscular bare back she was touching, that he didn't appear to have anything on!

'Do not be sorry, my sweet one,' Severo answered in a low tone. 'Who else would you come to in such a moment but your husband?'

Reggie would have moved her arms from him then. But a low rumble of thunder, sounding very much to her sensitive ears as though it was on its way back, had her hands gripping against him.

'I'm such a baby,' she groaned apologetically, and said no more because Severo had placed gentle lips against hers. It could have been a kiss of comfort—she wasn't sure.

'Your fear is understandable, little one,' he said softly, unhurriedly moving her as he spoke till she was lying on her back. 'It must have been a tremendous shock to your young system to have been in such an accident, apart from anything else.'

His hand had resumed its stroking of her arm, only this time it seemed to her to be more of a caress, and when thunder sounded to be coming closer, her hands clutched at the back of him, bringing his chest down against hers.

'Severo,' she gasped, this time not knowing if she called his name because of the thunder, or why . . .

'Shh!' he hushed her, and this time when his lips met hers, her own parted to meet them.

Then the thunder was in her heart, her heart thundering as though it would leap from her body. For Severo's caresses were becoming more intimate. The straps from her nightdress were slipped down her arms, her naked shoulders caressed, drawing a need from her to touch him, making her hands rove his back, an awareness of him as a man, as her husband, sending a thrill of sensuous pleasure through her, thoughts of where her actions were leading, her response to him, not touching her.

Then suddenly the lips that had been teasing hers alive were bringing a pressure to bear that told her, as well as the hand that left her shoulder and had her gasping as he touched her uncovered breast, that this was for real.

'Severo,' she breathed, but it was only a halfhearted protest, for his mouth had transferred to the hardened peak his hand had moments before captured, and as his lips moulded, embraced that sensitive area, she just had to hold him tightly, unable to deny the pleasure he was giving her.

When he found her nightdress an encumbrance, his hands moving upwards with the material against her leg, then thigh, her objection as she felt his hand on her hip had her halting him for the briefest of moments as he would have removed her covering.

'What is it, *querida*?' he asked softly, just as though he knew she wasn't really objecting at all.

'I . . .' She was swamped suddenly with shyness. 'Oh, Severo,' she said, 'I didn't mean to stop you,' and, glad of the darkness, for her colour was scarlet, 'It's just—I've never—been this way with a man before.'

She didn't know how she expected him to take that, but his hands left her body to come either side of her face, where gently he kissed her lips. 'You don't have to lie to me,' he said quietly as though he understood these things.

'I'm not lying, Severo.' Something in her voice, some honesty it would have been impossible to miss, had him still for tense seconds. 'You're the first man . . .'

She didn't finish. With a wondrous gladdened murmur of, 'Oh, *amor mío!*' Severo gathered her to him. And then with a tenderness, a gentleness she would have thought unbelievable had she not witnessed it at first hand from the tall, often aggressive, many times angry man she knew him to be, he set about making love to her in a way that had her enchanted.

Her nightdress had long since been dispensed with when with a touch that had her yearning for more his hands caressed her satiny skin and he whispered, oh, so gently, 'Your pain will be my pain, *querida.*' She knew then the moment to leave her girlhood behind had arrived. She raised her hands to his face and kissed him, letting him know that whatever happened in this new territory for her, she was totally in accord with wanting to be one with him.

CHAPTER TEN

LAST night's storm might never have been when Reggie awoke. From where she lay she could see a clear cloudless sky, sun streaming in through the window. She made no attempt to get up; she had realised at once that she was alone. She turned her head to see the dented pillow where Severo's head had lain, and a bemused expression settled on her face.

Never had she suspected such depths of tenderness in a man, such perfect understanding. What had happened between them, painful as Severo had intimated it would be, had also been something so privately beautiful, she just couldn't regret that it had happened. With her non-existent knowledge it had come to her that Severo was holding back the full power of the passion in him, unbelievably his first thought being to make it the wonderful thing it had been for her.

Alone, where only she could know such thoughts went on in her head, her colour came up as she found herself thinking—The next time . . . Then the door opened. She met Severo's gaze full on and her colour deepened further to a rosy pink that burned her cheeks.

Shyness had her eyes scurrying downwards before she could read the expression in his face. And she just had to wait for him to speak first in case she made a fool of herself by being nice to him, if he had returned to being the short-tempered brute he had been at dinner.

Her colour receded as the silence stretched, her expression going wooden that there was no spontaneous comment coming from him.

'So,' the silence was at last broken, but his tone was not very inviting, 'this morning you hate me, do you not?'

'Hate you?' Her face turned upwards, her eyes on his hard expression. 'Why should I hate you?' The query came quickly, and she coloured again, knowing full well to what he was referring.

'I see your memory is not at fault,' he said, observing her heightened colour and not having any trouble in knowing the cause for it. 'Do you not hate me, then, for making you forget your fear of thunderstorms?'

'The storm had passed over when . . .'

'The thunder had returned with even greater ferocity when I took from you what you were saving for dear Clive.'

Startled, she fixed her eyes on his, her mouth falling slightly open in wonder. Had she been so enraptured by his lovemaking that she had heard nothing except his gently encouraging words whispered close in her ear? Then his sour comment about her saving her virginity for Clive hit her, and her lips firmed.

About to fly at him, she checked. It had all been so new and beautiful for her, she couldn't, wouldn't, have it spoiled by an angry quarrelling with him. It was still new, precious somehow.

'I can't hate you for—for last night,' she told him quietly. 'To do so would mean I put the blame for what h-happened entirely on you.' She found it difficult to carry on, she had long since found the bed sheet of the utmost interest, but struggled on, 'Had I been myself I would never have come to your room, but I wasn't myself. I was half out of my mind with fear. I—I never gave thought to what might take place once I'd flung myself into your arms the way I did.'

She wished he would say something so she needn't go stumbling on. But from his silence, and she just couldn't look at him to see how he was taking what she was saying, it was left to her to show him she thought that if blame there was, then in fairness she accepted an equal portion.

'You—know now I knew little about—er—that sort of thing,' she said, trying not to get cross that he wasn't helping her out, 'but I know enough to know I created a situation a man would have to be a saint to ignore—clinging to you the way I did with—er—only my nightie on.' She stopped, knowing she was getting all round her neck with her vindication of him. Then thinking she had said more than enough, she lifted her head, and ended, 'You only meant to comfort me . . .'

'*Dios!*' The exclamation broke from him, the first thing he had said in an age. Then with a sardonic note of laughter, 'You think it was only for *your* comfort that I took you?'

The harshness of him had her sitting up, the sheet falling from her bare shoulders, his eyes on them reminding her what they both knew; that underneath the sheet she was naked.

'I . . .' She was lost for something to say in the confusion of knowing that from where he stood he could see what she had only just spotted, that her nightdress was on the floor in full view. He had known she hadn't a stitch on since he had first entered the room.

'For your information, little miss innocent,' said the man who had taken that innocence from her, 'the thunderstorm last night only precipitated my intentions.'

'P-precipitated?'

'It has been my intention to possess you from the moment I first laid eyes on you.'

If she had started this conversation by being totally honest, then it appeared Severo was treating her with the same courtesy. But what he was actually saying was taking an age to sink in.

'But—— ' her face was showing her puzzlement, 'but that wasn't in the agreement.' Then as shock took her and it came to her exactly what he meant, an awful letdown feeling came over her so that she might have broken down and wept had not anger come to stiffen her backbone. And then fury was spurting from her.

'So you wanted your money's worth! It wouldn't have mattered which one of us you took as your—*bed partner*—would it, Bella or me?' He went to interrupt her, but she felt too let down, too angry to let him. 'You'd agreed on ten thousand pounds for a wife—an English wife,' she corrected savagely, 'and you meant to have value for money right down to the last peso, didn't . . .'

'Your sister left me cold.' His anger flared, slicing through hers.

'Yet you would still have done to her what last night you did to me, what you've meant to do all along,' her fury refused to be shouted down.

'No.'

Just that one word, said quietly, but with such definite meaning to it, Reggie's anger dipped and she was confused once more. 'No?' she repeated, and was absolutely astounded when he explained that negative but loaded word.

'Aside from the fact that I never at any time had any intention of marrying your sister, her hard-eyed beauty left me cold.'

'*No intention of marrying her!*' She couldn't take it in. 'But—but the wedding date was fixed!' and, still gasping at what he had said, 'Abuela spoke of it that first time I saw her.'

'Marriage between your sister and me was never discussed,' he told her blatantly. 'I decided that *you* I would marry, and when—telling Abuela we had the night before set the date.'

For several long utterly confounded seconds, Reggie just sat and stared at him. Then red-hot fury like no other she had ever experienced stormed in.

'You *tricked* me!' came screaming from her.

'Are you saying you aren't glad I did?' he mocked, seemingly immune to her rage.

She was in so much of a lather then, not certain he wasn't referring to the joy he had given her in this very bed, or the fact that she had married herself to a wealthy rancher, that she only just remembered her nakedness. Unable to fly from the bed and scratch his eyes out, she looked for some solid object to hurl at him. The book she grabbed from the bedside table was a heavy tome, heavier than she had thought, but temper gave her strength for all her aim missed.

Having giving physical energy to her fury, she felt embarrassment oust it as with fiery eyes she followed Severo's kindling gaze. A horrified gasp left her as she saw the bed sheet, understandably, had slipped and she was sitting naked to the waist, her uplifted curves, rose-tipped breasts that had known his tender rousing to full-ness, exposed and being greatly admired.

'Don't waste all your heat in anger, *querida*,' Severo said softly, his temper gone as he appreciated what last night had been hidden in the darkness. 'I can think of a much better avenue to direct your fire.'

Cocooning herself in the sheet, Reggie heard the fish-wife in her screaming at him to, 'Get out!' and sat there seething when casually he picked the book up off the floor and placed it on the dressing-table, and as casually obeyed, his amusement getting the better of him in the deep sound of a laugh as the door closed.

'Vile pig!' she muttered, and continued laying her tongue to words that would have made her grandparents wince, for the five minutes or so that elapsed before a tap on the door showed Juana, looking not at all surprised to see her in the master's bed, bringing in a tray of tea.

Without embarrassment, which was more than could be said for Reggie, Juana picked up the nightdress from the floor and laid it on the bed, her eyes showing her happiness that the quarrel Maria thought had happened between master and mistress had been made up in a proper manner.

Reggie was still fuming after she had showered and dressed. She had no idea what Severo Cardenosa intended to do with his day, but it was for sure he wasn't going to spend it with her.

Deliberately she skipped breakfast, nor did she tell anyone where she was going. She wasn't sure herself. Certainly not to her favourite spot. If Severo came looking for her that would be the first place he would look.

Not wanting to use any of the normal exits where she might be seen leaving, she climbed easily out of her bed-room window, and furtively looked around. Making sure no one was about, she headed away from the *estancia*, for once unaware of the beauty that lived and breathed throughout the whole of Cerros de Cielo.

After walking for about an hour, she came to a dip in between two hills, and finding this the ideal hiding place, since no one would see her there not unless they climbed the first of the hills, she sat down with only a bumble-bee searching for nectar in the wild flowers for company.

To think she had been so ready to take her share of the blame! She had seen it as her fault for provoking Severo by her thinly clad femininity into making love to her. Yet all the time he had been waiting for such a moment. By his own admission, too, he had married her when that had *not* been part of the bargain he had made with Bella. Oh, how could she have been so green, so innocent! She had walked into his parlour every step of the way. The swine! She hadn't finished calling him names, not by a long chalk. He had known perfectly well she wouldn't contact Bella. She had trotted out too much information about Bella and James for him not to be certain of that—so certain that he had even had the nerve to point coolly to the telephone that day she had challenged him that marriage had not been part of the contract.

Oh, he was a swine all right. If it wasn't for Abuela she would pack her bags and leave right now. But he knew that too, didn't he! Reggie could have groaned out loud as she recalled the way she had told him she was fond of his grandmother—another little something to prick her conscience with should she step out of line.

For hours she stayed in her hidey-hole, her thoughts of Severo Cardenosa none the sweeter for the length of her stay. She still couldn't understand why he had married her when he had stated he had no such intention with Bella. Bella had hard eyes, he had said, though Reggie had never noticed they were hard. Did that mean, then, that her eyes were soft? That he had taken one look at her and had known straight away· that she was soft hearted too? Known that she could be easily manipulated where Bella could not? Decided that in his efforts to keep his grandmother happy he would marry a girl who was biddable, but not a girl like Bella?

Her head weary with her thoughts, she got to her feet. She could see the *estancia* from where she stood. It looked quiet and peaceful, and she was hungry. Weary though she was with having nothing but what Severo had revealed that morning going around and around in her head, she was still prodding at it as she made her way back to the house.

Severo had said he wanted to possess her from the first. What exactly did that mean? Reggie didn't kid herself she was any femme fatale, and with him believing—until last night, she amended, then hastily put last night out of her mind—that she had been with one other man at least, then he could have been forgiven for thinking he didn't have to marry her to get what he wanted. But why had he wanted her in the first place? He had said she was beautiful, but they rowed more often than not. Was that it? From the first they had flared up at each other. Did he not like his conquests easy? Had she fired a spark in him—and recalling that he had said something once about settling with her—had that been the devil that had driven him on to want to possess her?

Well, he had possessed her for the first and last time, she thought furiously. If he tried to come anywhere near her again he would soon find out she was nowhere near being settled with, nowhere near as biddable as he thought she was.

As she turned to go round to the front of the *estancia*, her eyes caught some movement. And then as she saw Severo, so deep in conversation with Manuela Gomez,

both of them entirely oblivious of her, she stopped dead
in her tracks, almost having to grip her stomach, so great
was the reaction there. An emotion took hold of her that
had her wanting to storm over to the pair of them, Severo
with his arm around Manuela, and tear his arm away
from her. To remind him that she was his wife, she,
Regina Cardenosa—she was the one who shared his
name, not Manuela Gomez; she was the one who had
shared his bed, not . . .

Reggie made it to her room barely knowing her feet
had left the ground as that sentence finished itself in her
brain. Everything, everything pointed to the fact that
Manuela Gomez had at one time shared Severo's bed—
possibly still did, if the way they had been lost to anyone
but their two selves out there was anything to go by.

And it was then, her appetite gone, that she realised
what the fierce feeling was that gripped her as she saw
Severo with his arms around Manuela Gomez. She was
jealous! So jealous she could have laid into the pair of
them. And as that knowledge sank in, she realised also
just why Severo had not had to use any persuasion to
make love to her last night. She was in love with him.

In love as she had never before been in love. All Clive's
persuasions to try and get her into bed with him had
failed—and she now knew why. She hadn't truly loved
him, not in the way she was in love with Severo. She had
given him her all, willingly.

Maria, coming to her room to remind her she had
eaten nothing all day, had Reggie sitting up on her bed
saying she'd had a headache, and when it looked as
though Maria would go rushing for the aspirin:

'It's better now, Maria.'

'You come to dinner now? Don Severo is not back yet.'

'He said he might be some time,' Reggie invented, not
knowing whose face she was saving, hers or Severo's.

Though since he hadn't bothered who saw him with his arms around Manuela Gomez, and she didn't need two guesses to know he was still with her, then he didn't seem to care what anyone thought of him.

Maria clucked disapprovingly that she only pecked at her meal, but had she known the effort it had taken to wash, change and come to the dining room at all, Reggie thought she might well have forgiven her.

At eleven o'clock there still was no sign of Severo. Reggie went to bed, burying her face in her pillow, the thoughts she had had that she would never again allow Severo to make love to her now seeming ridiculous. Why should he want to? She had negated any challenge if that was his sole reason in wanting to possess her, and anyway, Manuela Gomez was more than ready to take care of that side of things, by the look of it.

There was no chance of her going to sleep, but she did begin to feel better about the hopelessness of loving Severo when she recalled—and with it anger came to lift her leaden spirits—that he had declared, was it only yesterday, that he never broke his vows. What was he doing now, she would like to know, if he wasn't breaking that particular vow about keeping only unto her?

It had gone three when movement in the next room told her Severo was back. And I hope he's happy, she thought sourly, because she certainly wasn't. It wouldn't take too much effort to lie there and howl her eyes out.

It must have been about ten minutes later that she heard the communicating door between their two rooms open. The cheek of him! The utter gall! She was too incensed at the thought that at this late hour Severo had remembered he had a wife and was coming to check if all was well with her to think of pretending to be asleep.

'Our agreement was that you would knock before coming into my room,' she fired from her wide double bed, holding back the urge to hurl abuse at his head.

The room flooded with light as Severo saw no reason to talk in the dark since she was already awake. Reggie's heart thudded painfully to see him standing there, obviously showered wearing only his robe. Oh, how could she love such a man?

As an apology his mocking, 'Forgive me for forgetting to knock,' didn't get off the ground, 'but I rather thought we knew each other well enough to do away with that formality.'

His face took on a reminiscent look, and she had no trouble in following his line of thought. That he dared to refer to the way they had been last night, having just returned from *that* woman, doubly despoiled for her what had happened between them.

'Well, we don't,' she snapped, and, really on her high horse, 'And I should be obliged if you will kindly remember the arrangement we made and knock in future!'

His eyes narrowed as, propped casually against the wall, he looked across at her, her blonde hair tumbled about her head, her eyes almost navy in her emotional state.

'The arrangement *you* made,' he said slowly. 'You must forgive me again, but I have no recollection of agreeing to such an arrangement.'

Reggie found it impossible to remember whether he had or not, especially since from the look of it Severo wasn't ready to leave—more, she thought, looking ready to stay there all night playing this cat and mouse game.

'Well, in future,' she repeated stubbornly, 'knock. Or better still, don't come in at all.'

'Señora Cardenosa,' he said, more like a tiger waiting to spring than a cat, she thought, 'would you have me forget I have a wife?'

The nerve of him! The cool nerve of him! 'Forget you

have a wife?' she threw at him, sparks flying, shaking with fury as she grabbed for her watch. 'It's a quarter past three in the morning, and you talk of *remembering* you have a wife! You forgot that fact conveniently enough when you were with Manuela Gomez, didn't you?'

Oh, cool down, Reggie, cool down, you're in danger of saying too much, she thought immediately the words were from her. For Severo looked not at all put out at the words she was flinging at him. If anything he looked intrigued and—pleased? Mutinously she scowled at him, hating him at that moment that her reference to Manuela Gomez should remind him of his mistress and bring about that satisfied look.

'Jealous, my little spitting kitten?' he drawled.

'Don't flatter yourself! You can go where the hell you like—go now. And put the light out after you!'

Having shown him she didn't care a jot what he did, she presented him with her back, pulling the covers up over her ears. The light went out and she waited for the door to close, signalling his departure. But no sound came. What was he doing? She thought she heard him move. Where was he? Oh, what an idiot she was—she should have waited until he had gone. It wouldn't have taken a second for her to have nipped out of bed and put the light out herself.

When she felt the other side of the bed go down as if Severo had every intention of getting into bed with her, she was absolutely shattered. Without thinking about it she had turned over, pushing and shoving at him.

'Don't you dare!' she hissed.

For answer he grabbed neatly with one hand the two that were flailing him, forcing her, struggle though she might, until her back was against the mattress.

'Leave me alone!' she raged furiously, only to find that somehow he had them both beneath the covers, her hands coming into contact with naked skin, hair on his chest, telling her he had shed his robe.

'Ah, wife,' he said, his body weight over hers keeping her pressed immobile. 'What manner of woman is it who would allow her husband to shave at three o'clock in the morning and then try to eject him from her bed?'

'I didn't ask you to shave,' she grunted, still struggling. 'And you have no place in my bed either!'

His softly amused laughter as he told her, 'No man has more right, *querida*,' had her fighting him afresh.

'Will—you—leave,' she muttered through gritted teeth, frustrated that her efforts to oust him were meeting with so little success.

His reply was to bring his hands to cup her face—firm hands that held her head still as with unerring aim his lips found hers.

That first touch of his lips had a weakness growing inside of her, an inner self that wanted to respond. Then a picture of him with his arm around Manuela Gomez presented itself, and she was spitting fire and fury at him.

'No!' she screamed when his mouth left hers.

Then it was in silent combat that she fought not only against him, but as the picture of him and Manuela faded, against herself too, for he was raining kisses on her eyes, her ears, down the sides of her throat, without saying a word coaxing a traitor inside her into life.

And at last she was still. Part of her then wanted to say 'Don't, please don't, Severo, this isn't what I want.' But the other part of her, the traitorous part, was telling her that perhaps he hadn't been 'that way' with Manuela, and that now she wasn't fighting him he might just listen to her if she told him this wasn't what she wanted. And as his hand came to gently caress her breast, fanning the fire inside her into flame, Reggie opened her mouth.

'Oh, Severo,' she moaned.

'What is it, *querida*?' Oh, so soft his voice, a tenderness there so much like the tone he had used when last night he had taken her to paradise and beyond. She was lost.

She almost said, 'I love you' but found she was too shy to bring the words out. 'I—can't help myself,' she sighed.

'*Querida!*'

His longing for her seemed as great as her need for him in that one word. But it was without haste he removed her nightdress, and it was without pain that he made love to her. A union in which, as passion spiralled upwards, he revealed a furnace he had damped down to take her innocence—finding she had a passion to meet his—she knew if last night had been paradise, then she was at a loss to have said what this was.

She awoke after only a short sleep, maybe something in her subconsciousness taking sleep from her. She was still in Severo's arms, his even breathing telling her he was asleep. When half an hour later sleep again claimed her, there were tears on her lashes to tell her thoughts had not been happy ones.

Severo had gone the next time Reggie awakened. She hadn't felt him take his arms from her and leave, but she was glad he had gone. The rapture had vanished, leaving bitter humiliation in its place. It had come to her in her earlier waking that if she stayed with him she would reap again and again that same humiliation.

How could she continue to live with a man who stayed out until three in the morning with another woman? And, by now fully acquainted with the treachery of her own body, how could she continue to sleep with Severo? For though in the cold light of day she might tell herself it would never happen again, with the feeling she had for him, the feeling he could awaken in her, fight like she had done last night, it would happen again, she knew it. How could she live with herself? To awaken each morning afterwards and feel like this?

Her decision to leave him was only half made when Juana brought in her tray. Wanting to know Severo's whereabouts, as casually as she could Reggie asked Juana if she had seen him.

Juana's reply had her turning away so the young maid should not see her face. But it wasn't anger that beset Reggie this time on hearing that Severo had gone to the Gomez place, but defeat.

'*Gracias*, Juana,' she said, turning with a smile.

No one was going to know that Juana's words had left her with no alternative but to leave. She couldn't herself face yet that after the passion she and Severo had shared last night, his first action this morning was to go and see Manuela Gomez, his mistress.

'I shall not require your assistance this morning,' she told the girl in her improving Spanish. 'Perhaps Maria could do with some help.'

CHAPTER ELEVEN

HER heart aching, knowing to see Severo again would only add to her pain, Reggie hastily threw her things into her cases and tried to be practical. She would have to take the Mini; she might well need to sell it. Without humour the thought reached her that this was growing into quite a habit—selling Minis to pay her air fare. She still had the money left over from her wedding dress, but she didn't think it would stretch that far.

Writing a note to Severo she found her biggest obstacle. Though she was anxious to be away now the decision had been made for her, she found it irksome that emotion came time and again to cloud her thinking and delay her.

In the end emotion had to be banished, and it was a cold note she left propped up on the dressing-table, a note that made no mention of the real reason for her leaving, but merely pointed out that since Severo had tricked her into marriage she now considered, as in all fairness he must, that any hold he had on her sister must now be cancelled out. If he wished he could tell his grandmother that she had received a telephone call from England saying her sister was ill.

Hoping to leave the *estancia* unobserved, she decided she would take the rear way out. It had the added advantage of being nearer to the garages.

Breathing a sigh of relief that no one was about, she put her cases into the hall, quietly closed her bedroom door, then went swiftly to turn where the hall angled. There she stopped dead. She could hear Severo's voice!

Oh God, he was supposed to be out! The sound of a door opening somewhere behind her had her knowing she was committed. She had to move into the hall where Severo had his study or the person coming from that door would see her, suitcases in hand.

Tiptoeing like a thief in the night up to the open study door, her heart threatening to crack her ribs, Reggie approached the door, relief uppermost to see that while speaking on the telephone Severo had his back towards her. Then, terrified his ears would pick up the slightest noise, though his concentration seemed centred on what he was saying, she scooted past, not drawing another free breath until she and the Mini were heading down the drive.

She had gone five miles before what Severo had been saying on the phone separated itself from the other thoughts that were fighting for precedence. And then what he had said, the part she had heard, had her pulling over while on top of everything else her mind tried to cope with the enormity of it.

If she wasn't mistaken, and she understood his Spanish better than she did anyone's, then Severo had been agreeing with someone that he was facing financial ruin!

Oh no! Not Severo! Not with his pride! Who had he been talking with? His bank manager? Possibly, though that wasn't important. She had no way of knowing what his bank manager had said, but with an ache in her heart for him, all other pain forgotten, she could recall clearly his deadly serious voice as he'd said, '. . . the books tell their own story, don't they?' A pause, and she might have missed something, then, 'Yes, I have to agree—yes, it's the only way.' She couldn't remember the next bit and wished she had listened closer, but it had been something about impossible to stay afloat with the drop in cattle prices, the herd would have to go.

Stunned, disbelieving, Reggie sat trying to take in that the thousands of cattle she had seen just weren't a paying proposition. It seemed impossible that the well run, to anyone's eyes affluent *estancia*, could be broke. Yet with Severo talking of cattle prices dropping and that final agreeing that their herd would have to go, it just had to be so.

Oh, poor Severo, poor beloved Severo! What must he be going through? Never a word had he breathed to her. His pride, of course. That same pride, love and pride, she amended, that even while knowing how bad things were he must have added to his overdraft to have given Bella ten thousand pounds in order to make his grandfather's dying days happy. Oh, to be loved by Severo so much that he let his heart rule his head!

But she mustn't think of herself. Severo was the one in trouble. The blow to his pride would be tremendous, that blow added to when it became known that his wife of less than a week had left him. Loving him as she did, her own pride disappeared without trace. She had to go back. Severo was in trouble. It was as simple as that.

She turned the Mini round, the car he had purchased for her when he had known he was on the verge of ruin, but had bought for her just the same so that the people he employed should not wonder at the lack of a wedding gift.

And she had been thinking of selling it, she thought, as she turned into the approach to the drive. Well, it would have to go now, as would Severo's Maserati. Everything would have to go to clear the debts, as debts there must be, with the bank manager ringing him so early in the day. And when that was done, she would stay on, work beside Severo. Between them they would get the *estancia* back on its feet. Pray God he hadn't been into her room and seen the note she had left him. That was the first thing she must do, go to her room and tear up that letter.

She scarcely gave thought to the fact she was only supposed to be there for as long as they had Abuela. If she could help Severo she would stay as long as she was needed.

The Mini had just started its journey up the drive proper when Severo's Maserati came roaring down to meet it. Reggie's heart began racing as in seconds, his face taut and grim, Severo was up to her, brakes being applied with a force that left rubber on the driveway. Her first impulse had been to stop, her foot was already off the accelerator. But when Severo flung open his car door, his face like some demon, looking ready to leap and drag her out of her car, her foot went down on the accelerator again, hard.

Oh, my God, he's found my note, whipped through her thudding brain. Found it, probably checked her wardrobes too and found them empty, and by the look it being the last straw to his pride that on top of everythin else, when the state of the finances of the Estancia de Cardenosa became known, as they surely would when there were no cattle to be seen roaming his land, then everyone would think they knew why his bride of such a brief duration had deserted him. That she had married him only for his money.

The Maserati was riding on her bumper when Reggie pulled up at the *estancia*, a tight-lipped Severo more enraged than she had ever seen him yanking the door open before she had time to turn off the engine. It was he who cut the engine, taking the keys out of the ignition as if he intended never to let her have them back if this was the sort of trick she pulled.

Then she was being hauled out of the car, dragged round to the trunk, confirmation coming before the trunk lid went crashing up that her note had been read and he knew her suitcases were in there. Then while she was still trying to find some word that might take some of the steam out of him, he had her cases one under an arm, one in his hand and her in his other hand, the force of his grip hurting as he marched her inside the house.

'Severo——' she tried as she galloped to keep up with him, but she was ignored and had to swallow the fact that it looked as if he was in no mood to sort her out until they were sure of privacy.

It was to her room that he towed her. And once there, the door slammed hard shut, her cases went whizzing across the floor. Then he pulled her round to face him.

'As soon as I have finished with you you can unpack that little lot,' he said between clenched teeth. 'But first you can tell me what the *hell* you think you're playing at.'

To say that his expression, the volcanic heat in him terrified her, was an understatement, but she had to try to hide her fear, try to get through to him.

'You saw my note,' she tried, hoping that might explain everything.'

Pride—pride of possession was on his face, his words clipped as he bit, 'Did you think I would ever let you go?'

As she had thought he wouldn't stand to have gossiping tongues clacking behind his back.

'You—were coming after me?'

'You are mine,' he rapped, as if that said it all.

Reggie knew she would fare much better if she just agreed with everything he said; he had enough on his plate without this. But he was firing her to argue, stabbing at her streak of independence.

'I belong to me—no one else.'

'You are my wife,' he stated aggressively, thrusting her away when he next spoke as though to check himself from doing her physical harm. 'Did you think I would tolerate you leaving me for another man?'

'Another man?' She was gasping at the construction he had put on her note.

'Do you deny you have thought of little else but going to the man you love since receiving his letter telling you he would soon be free?'

Hot words spurted from her. 'Yes, I do deny it,' she said angrily.

She might well have saved her breath. She could see he didn't believe her, that her getting angry was doing nothing to cool his temper. Then she saw his eyes narrow shrewdly a couple of seconds before he barked:

'Don't dare lie to me! You were on your way to go to him when you changed your mind—when it came to you that the pickings would be better if you stayed with me.'

This final insult was too much. Reggie forgot completely then that it was purely his pride talking, for what pickings would there be if the *estancia* was on its uppers—though of course he didn't know that she knew that—and she had moved that step towards him with her hand flying through the air.

'You pig,' she yelled, her temper not alleviated that he

caught her wrist in a cruel grip that stopped her blow
from landing, her fury out of control that he should dare
to accuse her of wanting another man when he had a
load of dirty linen himself that could do with an airing.
'How dare you accuse me—when your own backyard
would take a year to clear up!'

'Backyard?'

His fury had been more than a match for hers, but
though he still held her wrist fiercely, the edge seemed to
go off it as his puzzled question hung there.

But if the edge had gone off his fury, then Reggie was
still livid. At some pain to herself she tore her wrist out of
his grasp, her eyes flashing.

'You were right not to believe my note,' she said furiously, careless that his lips had tightened ominously so
that it looked as though his interpretation of her letter
had been right, until she charged on, too angry to pick
her words. 'I was leaving because I happen to hold stan-
dards of decency you would know nothing of.'

'Decency?' He sounded baffled, but he knew what she
was talking about all right.

'At least I didn't know Clive was married when I
started going out with him.'

The narrowing of his eyes told her he had caught up
with her, an arrogance coming to him that didn't fool her
for a minute. 'Are you suggesting that I am practising a
little dalliance with a married lady?'

The utter nerve of him! To stand there, proud, arrogant, just as though he was as white as the driven snow!
He went farther.

'Perhaps you will be good enough to let me know this
married lady's name?'

'As if you didn't know!' she fairly exploded. 'Manuela
Gomez—that's who I'm talking about.' Her control on
her tongue had gone completely as the humiliation she

had felt on waking was recalled. 'Did you think I wouldn't guess after seeing you with your arm around her yesterday where you were last night?'

The words left her without regret. But far from looking furious at being taken to task by a shrewish woman he didn't care twopence about, Severo, with one of those lightning changes of mood Reggie never had been able to keep up with, seemed to lose the anger that had been violent in him, and did nothing to abate her own anger by appearing to quite enjoy the accusation she was flinging at him. As she was about to go for him again, his voice, silky this time, stopped her.

'You *are* jealous,' he said, and even had the audacity to grin as he said it.

'No, I am *not*,' she lied hotly, feeling more upset than ever that not only did he like the idea of her being jealous, but worse than that, he wasn't bothering to deny that he had been with Manuela last night. 'It—it's just that I've been brought up the old-fashioned way,' jealousy was sapping her anger, 'and . . . and I find it humiliating that you can come straight from her arms and . . . and then . . .' Her voice petered out, humiliation with her again.

'And come to the bed of my wife to enjoy the warmth of her newly awakened passion.' Severo didn't have the trouble she had in finishing it.

The memory of being naked in his arms had colour stealing over her otherwise pale cheeks. She didn't want Severo touching her, but seeing her blush and, guessing the reason for it she didn't doubt, he put his arms round her, charging her emotions as gently he kissed first one crimson cheek and then the other.

'You enjoy lying in my arms, do you not, *querida*?' he asked softly, the answer to which he already knew, she thought, already so aware of him that what powers of logic she had were already leaving.

As they left you last night, a voice within her was struggling to be heard. And then she was pushing at him, trying to get out of those arms when perhaps her mind would clear.

To her surprise, without argument, he let her go. 'You are not ready yet to be taken on that voyage of discovery we made last night,' he said, the gentleness in his voice making her forget for the moment that she had decided that morning that it was never going to happen again. 'There is so much I want to teach you . . .'

'We have to talk.' Firmly she cut him off; she had to, his very tone was seducing her, she had to stop it now— stop it before the urge to find out what more he had to teach could get a hold.

'Very well,' he said quietly, and while she sought round for the right words, feeling selfconscious suddenly, he said not another word, but waited to hear what she had to say.

Reggie knew she had to be very careful. She had to deliver what she had to say without heat, make sure she didn't say one wrong word. For if Severo reacted angrily, then temper that only he seemed capable of arousing— past her understanding when she loved him so much— would get out of hand, and who knew what she might reveal.

She took a deep breath, saw he was looking a model of patience, sincerely hoped he would remain so until she had finished, and was ready.

'My real reason for leaving you was because of what's going on between you and Manuela Gomez.' His right eyebrow ascended, but he didn't interrupt. 'I'm not judging you,' she declared, 'only stating the facts as I know them.' God, she sounded prim, and she could well have done without his smooth insertion:

'Do carry on.'

She hadn't missed that there was an edge of sarcasm creeping into his voice, but forcing herself to sound calm, no matter how she was inwardly feeling, she continued.

'You said earlier that you thought I changed my mind about leaving you because I thought I would be on to a better thing with you than with Clive . . .'

'So?' he prompted, a hardness coming to his voice that she had hoped not to hear.

'Oh, Severo,' she cried, knowing that since he wasn't going to bend his pride and tell her of his financial circumstances, then she was going to have to tell him about the phone call she had overheard. 'Severo,' she said, sick inside that she was about to topple his mammoth Uruguayan pride, 'I know,' she said gently.

'You know?' He sounded mystified. 'What exactly is it that you know?'

So he intended to keep up the pretence that nothing was wrong. With an ache in her heart for him, she whispered, 'I know that you're facing ruin.'

'*Ruin?*'

His acting ability was brilliant, she had to give him that. The surprise in his voice, the astounded look were masterly. She had to look away, unable to watch when his pride crumbled.

'I—overheard you on the phone not an hour ago,' she said dully.

He didn't answer, and she just had to look at him then. But his expression was not the one of destroyed pride she had expected, but was shuttered, telling her nothing except that he had recalled his telephone conversation.

'I was speaking in Spanish,' he said at length, and what was going on in his head she would dearly loved to know, if by so knowing she could help him over this most difficult of moments. For from that shrewd look in his eyes something was definitely going on in there.

'I know. But I know enough Spanish now to understand what was being said.'

'I see,' he said thoughtfully, then, 'Perhaps you would refresh my memory—tell me exactly what it was I said.'

'Oh, Severo,' she said helplessly, feeling to do so would be like rubbing salt in his wounds.

'Tell me,' he ordered sharply.

'Well,' it had been a command, and since he was insisting, 'I don't know who you were speaking with, your bank probably,' and when he neither confirmed or denied her assumption, 'but—but I heard you say the herd would have to go, that—that it was impossible to stay afloat, and—and something about staring ruin in the face,' she ended miserably.

'What else?'

'I didn't stay to hear any more.'

'You came straight to this room to pack.' His anger had returned full force, aggression biting. 'You decided on that instant that living with a man you hate was fine so long as his pockets were well lined, but that nothing would induce you to stay once you knew he was insolvent.'

Fury she didn't want was clawing for freedom at knowing just what he thought of her. It loosened her tongue and had words coming boiling from her.

'I've told you my reason for leaving,' she spat at him. 'I was *already packed* and on my way out when I saw the back of you in your study.' And, angrier still the more she thought about it, 'You have such a high opinion of me it just wouldn't dawn on you, would it, that once I'd had a chance to realise what the collapse of the *estancia* would mean to you—on top of that—the blow to your pride to have me walk out after less than a week of marriage, that I should decide to come back. Decide to work alongside you, to build again, to try and make the Estancia de Cardenosa what it was before.'

She still had plenty to fling at him, but the look of incredulity that had come to him stopped her. Well, she thought, not ready to forgive him for the light in which he saw her, he would look incredulous, wouldn't he? It would come as a mighty shock to him to know that far from her being the girl he thought she was, it didn't matter a brass farthing to her that he was penniless.

She hadn't expected him to thank her, she didn't want his thanks. But she was the one to be surprised when instead of referring to what she had just said, slowly, his face deadly serious, he asked:

'You don't hate me, Reggie?'

This was dangerous territory, she knew it, but since hate was streets away from love, she answered truthfully, woodenly, 'Of course I don't hate you.' And, all too conscious of the intent way he was looking at her, she got herself hopelessly muddled by adding, when she should have kept quiet, 'Do you think I could respond to you . . .' Oh hell, his silence was forcing her to go on, 'the way I did if—I hated—you?'

And suddenly Severo's mood had changed again, to her bewilderment becoming as lighthearted as she had ever seen him.

'I had hoped it was because you found me irresistible,' he said, and she saw from the look in his brilliantly blue eyes that he was highly pleased about something. Then his good spirits were hidden as he saw she was determined not to be amused.

'So,' he said, when he saw she was just as determined not to answer him, 'you are staying with me so that the Estancia de Cardenosa shall one day be as it appears to be now.' She still wasn't answering, for all he waited for her reply. She had said too much as it was. Then softly he was questioning, 'And what about my—affair—with Manuela Gomez? Are you going to accept that I have a wife and need a mistress too?' He couldn't have said anything more guaranteed to loosen her tongue.

'No,' shot from her. Then gathering her small control, stonily, and painfully, she told him, 'While you're seeing her I shall expect you to do me the courtesy of—not coming to my bed.'

His face was entirely serious when he answered, 'And what if I am not having an affair with Manuela Gomez?' This time he wasn't waiting for her answer. 'What if I tell you I have never had an affair with Manuela Gomez? And what if I told you that Manuela Gomez, for all her charms, leaves me as cold as your sister's hard-eyed beauty? What then, *querida*—would I then be welcome in your bed?'

Reggie was gasping at what he was saying. 'I . . .' she faltered. 'But—you are having an affair . . .' The arrogant look silenced her.

'Never once have I touched that woman in the way you suggest,' he told her sternly, then suddenly, for all he was watching her like a hawk, his expression eased. 'Though I will own to catching a glimpse of you looking particularly tight-lipped on the occasion I introduced the two of you. I will own too that I wasn't averse to wanting you to be jealous.'

Jealous! If only he knew. 'But—why?' she asked, too busy wanting to believe he wasn't lying when he said Manuela Gomez left him cold to get to the answer by herself.

'Why, *cara mia*?' Severo allowed himself a smile that included her. 'Because I have been insanely jealous of the man you told me you loved and couldn't see any reason why you should not feel some of the same when on that first meeting it looked as though you objected to Manuela.'

'Oh,' she said, her heart thumping, her face growing pink. 'Er—you have been jealous of Clive?'

'As jealous as hell,' he admitted unashamedly.

It wasn't very nice to be so pleased about his suffering, she had to own, but she couldn't help being pleased he had been jealous, any more than she could stop her lips and eyes from beaming a smile to him as she confessed:

'I discovered when I received Clive's letter that it wasn't true love I felt for him.'

With a warm look in his eyes just for her, a smile on his lips, he gently pulled her unresisting body into his arms. 'So that was the reason you looked so shocked.' Then his arms tightened about her as he asked softly, 'Was that when you discovered it was true love you felt for me?'

Without thinking she whispered, 'No, not then,' and immediately realised that what she had said amounted to a confession that she had at some time discovered that she did love him. 'Oh!' she said, scarlet, her eyes glued to the buttons down the front of his shirt.

But his shout of triumph, his hand coming to lift her face where he could see into her eyes, and the way he smothered her face in light feathery kisses, told her she had no need to be anxious, before he looked deeply into her eyes and told her:

'Regina Cardenosa, I fell in love with you within the first few minutes of meeting you.'

Holding on tightly, Reggie just looked back at him, her eyes shining. Then she swallowed, and just had to say, 'You didn't?'

'I couldn't help myself, *querida*,' he told her, gently kissing the wing of one eyebrow. 'I had come to Montevideo only to tell the Regina Barrington I knew that her services were no longer required, to tell her to go back to England. And then I met a Regina Barrington with soft, gentle eyes. Within minutes I knew you were the reason I had avoided marriage to anyone else—the reason I had held out against my grandfather's dearest wish to see me married and raise an heir.'

Stunned that he had loved her from the beginning, all Reggie was capable of at that moment was of staring at him. And as he saw her wide-eyed incredulity, Severo laughed, exultant to have her in his arms. His head coming down had her lips eager to meet the warm mouth that settled over hers. But the emotion he aroused in her did nothing to help her with clear thought, nor, when he at last pulled back, the long and loving look into her totally bemused face.

'Oh, Severo,' was all she was able to say, then as what else he had said began to penetrate, 'You were really going to send Bella back to England?' and at his quiet nod she remembered his delay in coming to Montevideo had been because his grandfather had died. 'But wouldn't you have brought Bella here for the same reason you brought me—for Abuela's sake, so that Abuela's last months should be . . .'

'*Amor mio*, I brought you here for one reason only, because I fell in love with you and had every intention of marrying you.'

'But—Abuela,' she began, finding it unbelievable. 'With your grandmother being so—frail—she must have been part of your reason.'

'Only in so far as I had already discovered a tenderness in you for your own grandparents, *querida*. It came to me then that if I could arouse some of that tenderness in you for my frail-looking Abuela then I knew I would have a basis to work on in my efforts to keep you by my side for ever.'

He delivered his confession without any sign of being abashed at the amount of emotional blackmail he had practised in that quarter, for clearly it had worked. And while Reggie was staring at him in amazement, he grinned endearingly and went on to tell her, to her further astonishment:

'Abuela is as strong as a horse. Sadness and shock at my grandfather's passing have made her wiry strength seem frail. But once she has made some adjustment to losing her beloved Roberto you will see a different Abuela.'

'It doesn't seem possible,' she gasped.

'Will you believe me if I tell you I had the doctor check her over only a week ago? He told me then that without question she should make her century.'

The news about Abuela had Reggie's full heart overflowing. She just had to cling on to Severo, feeling secure in arms that held her as though they would never let her go. For ageless moments he held her against a heart that beat loudly in her ear, telling of his deeply emotional feelings at that moment too. She would help him with the hurt that was his at having to lose his vast herd. He had told her once that her pain would be his pain. But now his pain would be her pain.

Bringing her head away from his chest, she looked into eyes that showed how deeply he loved her. 'We'll make it, darling,' she said chokily. 'We both have our health. One day the *estancia* will be the way it is now.' She stopped speaking when his hold on her tightened, seeing her words had aroused some seizing emotion his masculinity was trying to overcome.

'My beautiful woman,' Severo breathed, his voice thick so that he had to pause to clear it, his arms about her threatening to bruise her. 'To think I ever for one moment tormented myself into believing you were interested in my wealth! Instinct told me otherwise, the way it was so easy to work on your heart through Abuela.' He seemed to realise he was crushing her ribs and relaxed his hold slightly, but he just had to place a kiss on her lips before saying, 'I shall have to confess, much though I am falling more completely in love with you than ever with every misconception you utter.'

'Confess? Misconception?' Her puzzlement was evident.

'My true beloved,' Severo breathed tenderly, 'I'll grant your Spanish has improved. But as good as it is I'm afraid you are still missing the odd word spoken here and there, the inflection that can mean so much.' Seeing he had not helped to clear her puzzlement, he went on, 'Had you stayed eavesdropping a little longer on my conversation with Jorge Gomez . . .'

'Jorge Gomez?'

He grinned, then explained, 'I should have gone to see him this morning—I had left the house to do that, in fact. But the picture I carried with me—you looking so heart-stoppingly innocent, as beautiful asleep as you are awake, your hair tousled adorning your pillow,' he looked rueful, then added, 'hell, who could help but want to stay near to where you are?' Reggie didn't want to interrupt him—this was pure bliss. 'You, you enchantress, had me coming back into the house to see if my business with Jorge could be done over the phone.'

'Oh,' she said, not understanding at all, but unable just then to say anything brighter. Severo was making love to her with his eyes.

'You were right in thinking I was over at the Gomez home last night,' and at the slight stiffening of the pliable girl in his arms, 'You have no cause to be jealous, *cara mia*. I went only to see Jorge. He has been having problems for some time. Manuela confided in me some weeks ago. I wanted to do all I could, naturally, but he is a proud man, so helping him proved difficult. However, things came to a head yesterday with Manuela coming over in quite a state to say Jorge was positively suicidal.'

'That was why you had your arm around her.'

'I didn't know you had seen,' he said, regretful now that she had been hurt, then he went on, 'I couldn't do any other than go with her. When I got there I could see she hadn't been exaggerating. Jorge was on the verge of collapse with the weight of his worries.'

'Oh, the poor man!' Sympathy came pouring from her soft heart, and earned her a look of undying devotion. 'Were you able to help at all?'

'He is a proud man, as I said. All I was able to do to start with was to talk to him for hours on end. But at last he told me of his business problems and agreed I should go through his books to see if I could find anything he had missed. That took until the early hours of the morning.'

Reggie felt awful about the dreadful suspicions she had nursed and offered an instant apology which was accepted with a lingering kiss, before Severo pulled back and looked as though he would much prefer to be doing what he had than continue with what he had been saying.

'By the time I was through, Jorge was under the effects of a sleeping pill Manuela had slipped him—the first night's sleep he'd had in a week, apparently. Manuela had long since gone to bed, so I left a note to say I would be in touch this morning.'

'So you rang him . . .'

He nodded. 'While talking to Jorge yesterday I suggested an alternative if things were as black as he seemed to think they were. His night's sleep had helped to put things back into perspective, so that by the time I got through this morning he was already working on my suggestion. The conversation you overheard, *cara*, was me telling Jorge that though things were bad they weren't as bad as all that. I was agreeing with him that since there is a greater demand and a higher value being put on wool than cattle lately, his best bet was to get rid of his herd and change over to sheep—a good many ranchers in the same boat have made the change-over successfully.'

Amazed that she had got it all so wrong, Reggie just stared as what he was telling her began to sink in. 'Then—then it isn't you who's facing financial ruin, but . . .'

She didn't get to finish. 'Do you mind, *querida*?' he asked, gently teasing.

'Oh no, I'm glad,' she whispered happily, then quickly, 'Not because you're still wealthy, I mean . . .' She stopped, his look telling her he knew what she meant. Then, her brain going into action again, 'But if cattle prices have dropped, won't it affect you?'

'My herd is one of the best,' he told her without boasting, and remembering he had said something about his plan of selective breeding one time, she knew it for a fact. 'But should prices drop even further I have other interests which can sustain any loss.'

'Oh,' she said, as the full impact of what he was saying reached her. He was as wealthy as she had previously supposed, her help in getting the *estancia* back on its feet would not be required.

As though he read what was going through her mind and was aware of the slight feeling of disappointment that she had nothing to contribute, Severo brought one hand up to gently touch the side of her face as he told her, sincerity in every word:

'But with all my assets, all my wealth, I would indeed be very poor, my wife, without you here beside me.' Then tenderly he kissed her.

Looking at her adoringly when their kiss ended, he saw her glance jerk to the window when a rumble of thunder was heard. As he read her fear his hand came again to the side of her face.

'I love you, *cara esposa*,' he said tenderly, a new light kindling his eyes with the words 'dear wife'. 'Shall we again forget the *tormenta*?'

Shyly Reggie looked back. She felt his hands at the front fastening of her dress while their eyes held, colour coming to her cheeks as her dress fell to the floor. She saw the warmth of his smile break through that she was still shy with him, then he had picked her up in strong arms and was carrying her to the bed. Thunder was forgotten when he lay down with her—all her dark clouds had rolled away.

THE ALLURE OF URUGUAY

Uruguay is a fairy-tale land of rolling grassy plains, lush
with exotic flora and fauna and threaded with crystal-clear
streams. Approximately the size of England and Wales, it
is the smallest Hispanic country in South America. Brazil
and Argentina flank its northern and western borders
respectively, while in the south and east, the Atlantic
Ocean washes its two-hundred mile coastline of tiny bays
and intimate sandy beaches.

More than half of Uruguay's three million people
live in the elegant bustling capital of Montevideo.
Influenced by early European—mostly Spanish and
Portuguese—settlers, the city retains a distinct colonial
flavor, evidenced by its white, flat-roofed houses, wide
avenues and tree-lined streets. Spacious parks and gardens
abound; perhaps the most splendid is El Prado, where
strollers are captivated by the beauty and fragrance of
more than eight hundred varieties of roses.

Not surprisingly, one of Uruguay's major sources of
revenue is tourism. Visitors can explore the grasslands of
cattle and sheep country; luxuriate in the healing waters of
the famous thermal baths of Termas del Arapey; swim and
sunbathe at one of the many coastal resorts; shop in the
towns and cities for leather goods and topaz and amethyst
jewelry; gamble at a casino; and dine at any number of
excellent restaurants offering superb local cuisine.

Exceedingly rich in culture and history, Uruguay is a
land of excitement and beauty, the perfect spot for a
holiday... the perfect setting for a romance!

FREE!

A hardcover Romance Treasury volume
containing 3 treasured works of romance
by 3 outstanding Harlequin authors . . .

. . . as your introduction to Harlequin's
Romance Treasury subscription plan!

Romance Treasury

. . . almost 600 pages of exciting romance reading
every month at the low cost of $6.97 a volume!

A wonderful way to collect many of Harlequin's most beautiful love
stories, all originally published in the late '60s and early '70s.
Each value-packed volume, bound in a distinctive gold-embossed
leatherette case and wrapped in a colorfully illustrated dust jacket,
contains . . .
- 3 full-length novels by 3 world-famous authors of romance fiction
- a unique illustration for every novel
- the elegant touch of a delicate bound-in ribbon bookmark . . .
  and much, much more!

Romance Treasury

. . . for a library of romance you'll treasure forever!

Complete and mail today the FREE gift certificate and subscription
reservation on the following page.

Romance Treasury

An exciting opportunity to collect treasured works of romance! Almost 600 pages of exciting romance reading in each beautifully bound hardcover volume!

You may cancel your subscription whenever you wish! You don't have to buy any minimum number of volumes. Whenever you decide to stop your subscription just drop us a line and we'll cancel all further shipments.

FREE GIFT!
Certificate and Subscription Reservation

Mail this coupon today to
Harlequin Reader Service

In the U.S.A.	In Canada
1440 South Priest Drive	649 Ontario Street
Tempe, AZ 85281	Stratford, Ontario N5A 6W2

Please send me my FREE Romance Treasury volume. Also, reserve a subscription to the new Romance Treasury published every month. Each month I will receive a Romance Treasury volume at the low price of $6.97 plus 75¢ for postage and handling (total—$7.72). There are no hidden charges. I am free to cancel at any time, but if I do, my FREE Romance Treasury volume is mine to keep, without any obligation.

NAME_____
(Please Print)

ADDRESS _____

CITY _____

STATE/PROV. _____

ZIP/POSTAL CODE _____

Offer expires June 30, 1982
Offer not valid to present subscribers.

D2446